Crossroads

CW00525396

INTERNATIONAL BESTSELLING AUTHOR

TK LAWYER

THIS BOOK IS A WORK OF FICTION. ANY
SIMILARITIES TO ANY PERSON, PLACE, OR
THEORY IS IN NO WAY INTENDED OR TO BE
INFERRED AS FACT OR REFERENCE.
THE WORK IS THE SINGULAR PROPERTY OF
THE AUTHOR. IT MAY NOT BE REPRODUCED
IN WHOLE OR PART WITHOUT PERMISSION,
UNLESS AS PART OF A REVIEW, INTERVIEW
OR PUBLIC PUSH OF THE WORK AND
CERTAIN OTHER NONCOMMERCIAL USES
PERMITTED BY COPYRIGHT LAW.
CONTAINS ADULT SITUATIONS. 17+ ONLY

MANUSCRIPT PREPARED BY
HANEY HAYES PROMOTIONS

©2020 LAWYER
ALL RIGHTS RESERVED

1 ~Marisole~

Marisole's eyebrows shot up. "I can't believe it!"

Paige shrugged her shoulders while her hands remained clasped together in her lap. "Why? What is there not to believe?"

Marisole threw her arms up in the air. "But Joey saw him? I mean, really saw him with his own eyeballs?"

"He walked in on them. Almost ran over them, as a matter of fact, trying to get to the floor cleaner bottle."

Marisole blew out a sigh of disgust. "Boy, I sure know how to pick them, don't I?"

"He wasn't worth it-you know. Darrell never deserved you. At least that's what Joey thinks. He wanted me to be the one to tell you."

"Sooo, you think Darrell deserved me?"

"I didn't say that. He was a jerk. A womanizer. No one deserves that."

Marisole tapped her fingers on the table. "Yeah. Break time's almost over. I gotta go."

"See you soon."

Marisole leaped up from her seat, shoved her lunch bag into her locker, straightened her blue colored vest, and then threw open the double doors to step onto the main floor. The holidays were no fun at work, but she needed the extra money. After her parents served her a contract outlining their strict rules for her post-secondary training, Marisole moved out of her parents' home and into a college dorm.

She only had one thing to say about the situation. Thank God for student loans! There was no way she would be able to afford the meal plan, much less the housing cost. The dorm is where Marisole met Paige, who became her roommate and now her buddy. They applied to one of the largest retail stores in the area and ended up being hired almost at the same time.

While Paige was strictly back of the house, Marisole took care of customers at the front end of the store. Although there were days, she craved hiding in the warehouse with her friend. The fact that Paige and Joey, her long-time friend, were now dating was... remarkable and incredible. Joey needed a Paige in his life a long time ago. She recalled the first time Joey looked at her roommate. From that moment, Marisole knew he was done for. With long blonde hair, pulled back in a braid and a svelte, athletic build, she knew Joey would fall for her. It was only a matter of time before he'd notice Marisole wasn't the only one in the room.

As happy as she was for them, she missed the days she had Joey all to herself. "You're the only one for me," he whispered to

Marisole, following up the sentiment with a deliberate wink. "I'm holding out for you," was another favorite of his he'd dish out while they were alone. Gone were the days he paid particular attention to Marisole. As soon as Paige walked into Marisole's dorm, Joey only had eyes for her.

Having known Joey all her life, Marisole knew he was a good man, and he deserved a good woman to share adventures with. Paige was it- at least for now. Who knew what lay in store for him after college?

Marisole considered why she didn't take a chance on Joey. The thought had crossed her mind several times, especially during those sad moments he held her in his arms because some louse broke her heart. She couldn't deny she loved him, but she couldn't get past the friendship part. Joey was not the right one for her. He was funny as hell, and his smile was cute and endearing. She'd do just about anything to catch his genuine, schoolboy grin. He also had the biggest heart and the warmest bear hug but *sexy?* Nah. That did not describe him at all, and Marisole wanted that. She wanted friendship; first and foremost because relationships between friends were so much nicer, but sexual attraction was good too. Over the years, as Joey developed into a capable, independent-minded man, she thought her feelings might change for him, but they never did. Joey was a friend, a good one, but that was all he would ever be.

Joey's best friend, however, was a different story. At six-foot, two inches tall with firm, lean thighs, broad shoulders, and a broad chest, Clay was an impossible Adonis. Sadly, every man came with flaws, and his were gigantic- massive ones she was ill-equipped for and incapable of tackling on her own.

Clay was a heartbreaker.

He was definitely not the man for her though one could dream. Hers were wet dreams, complete with Clay in the buff found in the strangest places, on and off-campus. While Clay never seemed to notice her, she couldn't help sneaking glances his way when he was around. Granted, he never came on campus to see her. He visited Joey. Clay was only recently introduced to Marisole.

Tomorrow night was the first on-campus party she and Joey were attending. She contemplated if Clay would be there, too? Though Clay didn't attend the same college they did, Joey often invited him to events he took part in. Would Clay attend alone or on the arm of a slim, tall waif? Clay's type never strayed, and his preferences did not include her own over-generous build. Though he dated young females, there was nothing else Marisole seemed to have in common with Clay's vast fan base.

Joey warned her about Clay, informing her that he had a wandering eye. Sadly, his gaze never lingered too long on her.

She sighed as she helped the next customer, rounding the edge of the counter to scan an item in their cart. On the way back to the register, she turned her left arm toward her, glancing down at her watch. An hour to go and she'd be free of this place. Homework awaited her rapt attention back at the dorm. Just when she thought she was almost in the clear, a warm body sidled up next to her, and a familiar voice said her name.

"I had a call out. Can you cover the next shift for a few hours?"

With her plans shot in less than a minute, she nodded as she finished up with the customer. The holidays were rough. Her homework would have to wait.

***

After surviving most of the day gulping down glasses filled with the caffeinated nectar of the Gods known as coffee, she turned in her book report. She prayed it was adequate enough for a victorious outcome. Getting home late last night did nothing to give her a jump start to the finish, yet she did all she could in the amount of time she had available. She only hoped it was enough to earn a "B" grade or better for the class.

Joey caught up to her and hugged her shoulders with one arm. "Hey!"

"Hey, yourself. Where's Paige?"

"I do have a life without her, you know."

She opened her mouth wide and teased, "Oh? One would never know."

His smile widened. "Jealous? If you want me, I'll drop her like a hot potato."

She laughed. "Oh no, you're not! She's the best thing that ever happened to you."

He winked. "I thought that was your job."

She lightly punched him in the arm. "You are too much."

He pointed at her while he ran backward toward a large white building. "That's what she says. I'll see you later, right?"

Marisole nodded and shouted at his disappearing form, "Yeah."

She re-focused her attention to the next task on her agenda. Waling up a long, metal ramp, she swung open the door to the large trailer temporarily housing the Women's Crisis Center. As soon as the campus leaders came up with the idea of assisting women in crisis situations with having a more successful college experience, Marisole signed up to volunteer. Maybe it was due to her personal experience with abuse. Helping others in her same situation or worse was not a question, it was her duty. Marisole believed in female empowerment. The more information she could give to a client, the better choices they could make for their future.

The verbal and emotional abuse her dad easily dispensed on her allowed her to empathize with the victims walking through the door. Some of them had experienced atrocities she would never understand, but all of them were the same. They all sought help and resources. That's what she imparted to them. To the best of her ability, every hour she worked.

If Clay could see her now, what would he think? Would it matter to him that she helped empower women to make informed choices?

Having a strong passion for strengthening women, she couldn't envision being with someone who didn't have the same fire within them. To work in the field and get paid, too, would be a dream come true. However, her dream job, at the crisis center didn't produce a paycheck, and she had student loans. After she graduated and paid off her massive debt, she would have to figure out a way to return to the work she dearly loved.

In the meantime, she didn't know what Clay thought about her volunteer work, and she didn't understand why she cared. He was likely with another woman at the moment if he wasn't attending classes. A year ahead of her and Joey, Clay was in college, too. He attended another university and lived in an apartment with roommates. Whether his roommates were female or not, she didn't know, but she wouldn't put it past him to collect a harem.

The door chime sounded, indicating her first customer arrived. She was happy for the reprieve from her busy thoughts. Striking the female's name from the sign-in log, she called out her name with a gentle smile plastered across her face and escorted the student to one of the few rooms in the back of the trailer.

She smiled at the tiny female seated across from her. "My name is Marisole. How can I help you?" And her day began.

***

Stepping through the intricately carved front door, Marisole was greeted with vibrant chatter and music blasting her sensitive eardrums. She swung her head left then right, scanning her immediate area. People lined almost every square inch of the room, some with drinks in their hands while others gestured wildly as they talked. She scanned the room seeking a familiar face. She kept walking, squeezing, and contorting her body in between people lazily scattered about the appetizers and punch bowl. Strolling aimlessly about the room, she ventured into another, her gaze straying toward the long stairway she assumed ended on a second floor. Where were they? Were they upstairs? The last thing she wanted was to walk in on Joey and Paige doing something she never cared to witness.

Unfamiliar faces greeted her as she passed by, some laughing and others smiling. Some of the strangers even waved. She swept up a tasty looking potsticker appetizer when she spotted Joey and Paige in the corner of the room. Thank God they hadn't found the bedrooms yet.

She acknowledged their presence as she walked toward them. "Hey, you two."

Paige looked up, first. "There you are. Joey and I were wondering if you were coming."

"Yeah, I said I would though part of me would rather be studying."

Paige raised an eyebrow and scanned her from head to toe. "You need to get out more often. Maybe I should hook you up with one of my friends."

Marisole shook her right hand in front of her, deflecting Paige's offer. "No, no, that's okay. I don't think I'm up for a blind date."

Paige focused her attention on Joey. "What do you think? Wouldn't Martin be a good match for her?"

He almost shouted his retort. "Him? God, no!"

"Why not?"

"Marisole's got too much class for him."

Paige swatted Joey's shoulder with a feigned look of shock. "Like Martin doesn't have class!"

"Look, I don't think he's good enough besides let Marisole find her own dates."

"Geez, okay. Just trying to help."

Marisole chuckled. "I'm good, but thanks. I know you mean well."

"Beer!" Someone shouted the word behind them, and a stampede erupted. Marisole watched as people from everywhere scattered about, aiming for the adjacent room where she assumed someone had brought a keg.

Joey looked over at Paige. "Should we join them?"

Paige shrugged her shoulders and licked her lips. "If you want. I'm good with this fruit punch. It's yummy, and no one's spiked it yet."

He lowered his head. "Come on. Let's go." He crooked his arm out for Paige to take and nodded toward Marisole. "We'll see you later."

She returned the nod, bending down to straighten her crumpled pant leg and considering what to do next now that Joey and Paige had abandoned her. She contemplated what to do with her free time as the sea of faces and bodies before her parted. Her head shot up as she spotted a familiar person leaning against the door frame.

Clay's smoldering gaze met hers.

He crooked up a gentle smile as she stared at him, frozen, unable to speak, move, or think. The man was smoking hot, and his smile warmed straight through her, sending tingles of joy and pleasure in areas she'd rather not disclose. His perfect, muscle-bound body, alone, drew any woman's attention. Still, for Marisole, it was his stellar, sweet smile that was the icing on the cake. She knew exactly how she wanted to enjoy the dessert, tempting her to take a bite, only a few feet away.

Did Clay realize how frustratingly sexy he was? From her short interactions with him, she detected no hint of an inflated ego, which went against everything she thought about good-looking men. The reality was, if Clay was self-inflated or self-absorbed in any way, he couldn't be Joey's friend. Joey wouldn't tolerate it. But, Clay was no friend of Joey's; he was his best friend, which said a lot about his character.

Marisole's gaze followed Clay's as he turned his head toward the woman tugging at his arm. It figured. He came with a date, or maybe he met her at the party? Regardless, it was a splash of harsh, wet, cold reality from the bucket of life for Marisole. She needed the reminder to squash the images of her and Clay in a relationship that would never happen.

The female next to Clay wore a crop top and fringed, striped shorts that went way up the middle of her thigh. Her abdominal was impeccably firm, and her curly dark hair looked cute, natural, and put together unlike Marisole's wild, dark brown locks. She glared at Marisole before ushering Clay into the other room.

Marisole folded her arms across her chest, crinkled her nose and murmured under her breath. "Wonder what that was all about?" She made her way to the appetizers and grabbed a glass of punch, sitting down on one end of a long couch with a plateful of food.

A freckled boy sat down next to her and smiled. "Hi." Well, maybe he wasn't a boy, but he sure looked like one. He was cute, though a bit young for her taste. He extended his hand out, balancing his paper plate with the other one. "My name's Ryan. What's yours?"

She shook his hand. "Marisole."

"So, what year are you in?"

"Junior, and you?"

"Freshman."

"Oh…" That explained the youthfulness.

He pointed at her. "I know you. Weren't you a volunteer at that fundraiser for the Crisis center? You know, the plant a tree event?"

She turned her head to one side. "Um yeah. Wait a minute. Were you there, too? You do look familiar."

"Yeah, I do a lot of volunteer work on campus."

She shared an enthusiastic grin. "So do I." When she turned to glance at the space Clay had abandoned, she found him again, watching her. Clay's eyes narrowed at her companion.

Ignoring Clay, she turned her attention back to Ryan. "Are you on the team for the cemetery cleanup?" When he nodded, she continued, "So, I guess I'll see you there."

Ryan grinned, his striking white teeth beaming within his smile. "If not sooner."

She shied away and gave him a small grin. Was he hinting at something more?

"Care for a dance?"

She wrinkled her nose. "In a frat house?"

He shrugged his shoulders. "Why not?"

She glanced up at Clay before responding, "Well, why not after all." Ryan helped her up from the couch. She was aware of Clay's attention on her as they skipped over to the dance floor. Where was the girl he was with earlier?

They gyrated in the middle of the other students. Making moves she knew wasn't part of any dance choreography. At least not at prestigious ones that she could claim. She let herself go, feeling the beat of the music within her bones, uncaring who witnessed her abandon. She closed her eyes and eased into the rock and roll sounds, sneaking a peek every once in a while to make sure she wasn't bumping into a fellow neighbor while getting her groove on. When she swung around, waving her hands in the air above her, she tipped to the left. Finding strong arms around her, steadying her back onto her feet. She laughed and opened her eyes, aware of her silliness as she lay against someone's firm, broad, and very masculine chest. It couldn't be Ryan, could it? Did he grow several inches taller in the past twenty minutes they were dancing? She laughed hysterically as she pictured it. Ryan's hairy head elongated and reaching for the sky, deforming him into a character from an old film she saw several years ago. Coneheads. Hilarious. Maybe someone had spiked her punch, after all. She shoved her hands against the cozy warmth that recently cradled her head, almost toppling backward when she found who held her in his arms. It wasn't Ryan. It was Clay.

"Careful. You like running into things, huh?" His deep-throated chuckle disarmed her. She stepped off the dance floor.

"You're welcome." Clay snorted and followed, shortly behind her.

She turned in mid-stride. "What are you...you...what are you doing on the dance floor next to me?"

He raised his eyebrows. "Oh, is the dance floor considered your property? I can't be near you?"

She pointed toward him. "You know what I mean."

"Apparently, I don't."

When Ryan suddenly stepped up to her, she made introductions then took off, seeking a place to sit or, better yet, add distance between her and Clay.

Clay shouted after her. "Are you walking away now? I just wanted to talk to you and get to know you."

She nibbled at her thumbnail. "Why?"

Ryan interjected, "Listen, I'll leave you two alone, but I wanted to get your number before I leave, that's if you're up for lunch or coffee some time?"

She glanced over at Clay then back at Ryan. "Sure, I'd love that." After exchanging numbers, Ryan promptly left. Marisole tilted her head and furrowed her eyebrows together, searching Clay's face for some clue as to what he was doing on the dance floor beside her. Clay extended his hand to her, and Marisole gasped.

"It's not a marriage proposal. I just wanted to let you know Joey and Paige left the party, and I wondered if you wanted to leave too? I wanted to talk to you and get to know you since you're a good friend of Joey's."

"Oh?"

He motioned his hand toward her again and grinned. "If you want to go, I can lead you out of this crazy place."

Lord. She could get lost in his soft, welcoming grin. She placed her small hand in his, relishing the mighty strength of his capable grip. Before she knew it, he wove a path through the half-drunken crowd, and the door closed behind them.

2 ~Clay~

Leading Marisole out the door was easier than he pictured. Images of the fiery female resisting his natural charm and blasting him with a stream of curse words, some she may have conjured up in the heat of the moment, plagued him. He watched her, and the skinny guy currently hitting on her, dancing. Well, at least she might've called his gyrations, dancing. What the guy did in the middle of a large crowd of onlookers was a bit awkward and beyond description. It was more like a throwback to the seventies or possibly a tribute to John Travolta.

Marisole's words interrupted his thoughts. "Wait. Where is the girl you were with? Shouldn't you be with her?" Her eyes widened, and her mouth closed, abruptly, as he turned toward her. "It's okay. I don't need to know what happened to her."

Marisole was a curiosity he couldn't let go of. She confused him, too. He could've sworn she was interested in him, for he caught her staring at him several times tonight. It wasn't only at the party where he found her sneaking peeks at him with those long, lush lashes that adorned her eyelids. She stole glances at him whenever he was around. He had dated plenty of women to know when one of them was giving him a sign. He wasn't wrong about her. Though she never took action, she had to have some interest in him.

Even if Marisole shared no concern for him, she fascinated him. A beautiful, strong female with a pleasing, curvy form- what was there not to like about Joey's friend? Clay wanted to know all about her, and since she didn't make a move to get to know him, he was taking the first step. The only problem was if things didn't work out between them, where would they be? Clay was jumping the gun, though, and he knew it. A few drinks and casual conversation did not make for a relationship no matter how much Clay wanted that with her. She spurred his libido, keeping him up at night when homework and the latest female entertainment kept his usual interest.

She rubbed her naked upper arms in an attempt to ward off a chill. "What do you want to talk about?" Her shoulders tightened as Clay slipped off his coat and swung it around her.

"Relax. I'm not that bad. You act like you're in trouble or something."

"Um, I'm just not in the habit of being whisked away by strange men."

He threw his head back and laughed. "Strange men? That's a first."

"Oh? None of your female friends ever call you that before?" She teased before her casual tone turned serious. "Sorry. Your love life has nothing to do with me."

He snorted. What love life? The females he bedded were strictly for entertainment purposes. They knew what they were getting into when they walked through his door. One night of mutual pleasure with the possibility of a few more dates, if he liked them. Sleepovers, meeting his roommates and a real, steady relationship was out of the picture. Until he found the one, he wasn't aiming to get serious.

They stopped at a railing lining the edge of a lake. Marisole placed her hands atop the cold metal while Clay leaned over the railing and looked down at the water. "You don't think much of me, do you?"

"Why would you say that?"

"Because you're always mentioning my female company, and I can tell by the tone of your voice that you don't think of them or me in high regard."

She sighed and shook her head. "That's not true. I have no business talking about the women you hang out with. Sorry. Sometimes my mouth runs away from me."

He smiled; his attention now focused on her saucy mouth. "I like a woman with an opinion."

She blinked and remained silent.

He changed the subject. "So... A Communications major? What do you plan to do with your degree after you graduate?"

"Not sure. I'm hoping to get into some type of management. I think that would be good for me and the best use of my major. I hear you're in Business Administration. I considered that once. Too much math."

He turned toward her. "I'm good at math. Not so much English. So, have any plans for Christmas? The holiday break is coming up, and the campus will be closed."

"I know. I'm not sure what to do, but I think Joey will let me stay over with his parents for a while, that's if Paige doesn't bombard his spare room." Marisole giggled.

"You can stay with me if no other options come up."

Her jaw dropped. "What? I don't know you, plus you have roommates."

"Two of them, and they will both be visiting relatives out of state." He leaned back on the railing. "I know you don't know me, but I am Joey's best friend. You can trust me. I would never let any harm come to you."

"The dorms will be closed for one week."

"Yeah."

"I can't impose on you for that long."

Clay turned back to the lake. He clasped his fingers and leaned his arms on the railing. "We'd have fun." When her eyebrows shot up, he realized how his suggestion came across. He replied quickly to correct his mistake. "I meant there are a lot of Holiday events happening that week, and I think it would be fun to spend that time with a friend."

"Don't you have friends?"

"I'm trying to get to know you. You're important to Joey, and anyone important to him is worth getting to know."

She glanced at the ground.

"Talk about it with Joey and come to some agreement. The last thing I want is for you to be stranded over Christmas break."

She opened her mouth to protest. "Oh, you know about the situation with my parents. Of course, Joey told you."

"And no one else. No one needs to know."

"Thank you."

He nodded. "You're welcome. I know it's an odd proposal but realize any friend of Joey's is a friend of mine. Friends help friends."

"I appreciate that. I'll discuss it with Joey."

"Let me walk you to your dorm."

"Again, thanks. You're too kind."

Marching up the few steps to her building, she turned the key in the lock and then pulled off his coat and handed it to him with a warm smile. He watched her as she strolled away from him, a sudden strange emptiness clouding his heart.

***

Joey shouted, "You offered her what?"

Clay took a step back as Joey moved to face him. "She's a good friend of yours, and I don't want her left behind to fend for herself in case she can't find a place to crash. You told me yourself, you were worried about her."

"Yes, but I didn't think you'd offer your apartment to her!"

"Look, I didn't know you were going to take it this way. I was only trying to be a friend."

"I understand, but it's just not a good combo. Did you consider your roommates?"

"They'll be gone." Clay threw his hands up in the air. "Come on, man, I'm not going to put her at risk, and you know it."

Joey's eyes narrowed. He pointed at Clay, tipping his own chin up, for emphasis, as he spoke. "Wait a minute. Something is going on here. You like her, don't you?"

Clay remained silent.

He shook his index finger at Clay. "No. No. No. You need to stay away from her."

Clay blew out an exasperated sigh. "Why does everyone think I'm a bad guy?"

"You're not, but you are bad news for her. You're not going to bed her and toss her out like you do with all your other women!"

"Oh, jeezus! Do you think I would do that to one of your good friends? I know how much she means to you." He blew out a breath of air and shook his head. "Tell me. If you feel this way about her, why haven't you dated her?"

Joey frowned. His eyes swept the floor. "She's not interested in me. Besides, I have Paige, and she's a good woman."

"Yeah. That she is." Clay slumped into the middle of the couch. He rested his head on the back of it and stretched his arms out to either side of him.

Joey took a seat directly in front of him. "So, what are you going to do?"

"I'm going to do the Cemetery clean up and go out with the twins tonight."

Joey rolled his eyes. "That's not what I meant. And the twins again, really?"

Clay crooked up a devilish smile. "Double the fun. Besides, you know each chick gets one chance with me. That's the least I can do." He winked.

Joey laughed. "Damn, I need to keep Marisole away from you."

"I would never treat her that way."

Joey leaned forward. "Is that because you like her?"

Clay scrubbed one hand over his chin stubble. "Probably need to clean up for them. Those two make a wild pair if you know what I mean."

Joey placed his hand on his forehead. "Okay, I get it, but I am not leaving you alone in the same room with Marisole, you hear me. If she stays with you, you better accommodate me too."

"Fine."

Joey lifted from the chair and made his way to the kitchen. "Good. Now, while I grab us some drinks, tell me about this girl you have on the side. What's her name? Tiffany?"

Clay smiled.

"What do you see in her?"

"We like to have fun. I can call her, and she can call me when we want..." He cleared his throat. "You know, company. We see each other at odd hours. My boys are fine with it, thank goodness because she can make quite the racket." He grinned.

"Goodness, and I'm supposed to trust you with my Marisole?"

Clay mumbled under his breath. "I already told you. It's different with her."

"So, how's the volunteer work going? I hear you are up for an award."

"Yeah. Volunteer of the year. I was nominated, and I might have a chance. I'm pretty proud of it."

Joey handed a glass to Clay. "You should be. You are out there helping the community. You know Marisole does that too. She's a feminist through and through. She truly believes a woman can do anything. You should see the spark in her eyes when she talks about her work. She has such a passion and drive for it."

"She does. I've seen it. That's what makes her special and different from the other women, Joey. I respect her drive and her passion. I can see why you're friends with her." Clay took a swig of his beverage and then dropped his glass onto a nearby coaster. "What I don't get is why she's single?"

Joey leaned forward on the sofa seat and clasped his hands in front of him. "She's tried, but she always ends up with losers. You know, she had a hard life with her mom and dad, especially the old man. He didn't treat her right, so she doesn't think much of herself. She comes off as confident and happy. You would never know there's sadness lying underneath."

While Joey spoke, Clay found himself propped up on the couch, staring in earnest and eager to know more about Marisole. What he said about her came as a surprise to him. What Clay witnessed, each time he saw her, was a happy, bubbly, beautiful female sharing giggles and exuding positive comments to all she knew. This darker side of her he did not know. It gave her depth of character. He itched to know who she was beyond the painted mask she left on for others.

"I've known her for years. She thinks she's fat and plain looking."

Clay shouted, his tone of voice escalating with his irritation. "Not true! She's beautiful!"

"I knew it! You do like her!"

Clay dropped his head. "Look, I got to go. I've got to get to the Cemetery clean up before they get started."

Joey lifted his glass as Clay stepped up to the door. "Alright, buddy, I'll see you soon."

Clay waved and shut the door behind him.

Driving to the cemetery, Clay chastised himself for being too honest with Joey. He was interested in Marisole, no doubt, but starting a serious relationship with someone at his young age? That wasn't happening. Why start something he wouldn't finish? He had a college degree to complete and a career to get started. Afterward, he might be interested in seeing where things went – with the right girl, that is- but for now, his future lay ahead of him, and casual dates were all he could spare in his free time.

Marisole deserved a devoted man whose attention revolved around her and her comfort. She needed a man who had the extra time to treat her as she deserved. Clay was honest when he said that she was special, for she was a real treasure, different than the girls he paired up with. She was not only stunningly beautiful but fiery and gracious at the same time. From what he knew about her, she wasn't afraid of honesty, and she lived her life with rare integrity that was hard to find anymore. She was gifted with the ability to frame difficult subjects in a kind but straightforward way. He loved that in a woman. She was deserving of a good man.

As he pulled in to an empty space, he grimaced, spotting Ryan hovering near Marisole. The boy was out to get her attention, and he wasn't going to take no for an answer. In Clay's opinion, the boy was way too young for Marisole, but then his opinion might be biased due to his mixed feelings for her. A web of confusing emotions he wouldn't exactly call affection but more like respect and a deep desire to get to know her better. Still, Marisole remained evasive in his attempts at learning more about her. Thank goodness for Joey. From the earful his best friend gave him this morning, he knew more about her now than he did when he woke up today.

Clay slammed the door and pulled out his work gloves from his back pocket. It was time he joined the others while simultaneously implementing a successful plan to thwart Ryan's romantic endeavors. Sporting a wicked smile, Clay took his first booted step onto the concrete sidewalk and moved toward the cleanup crew gathered under a large Oak tree.

***

Clay woke up with a smile plastered across his face. Not expecting the twins to come back to his place, he ended up with more than he bargained for. His balls ached as he recalled key moments last night in their stellar late-night rendezvous. Every second he spent in bed with them proved immensely satisfying. He moved his index finger through the air above him. Checking off the imaginary box in his head marked *"sex with twins"*- an otherworldly experience he never considered possible before. If he had a bucket list, he would never have listed this experience on it. What occurred last night, he figured, was a fantasy most men desired but rarely considered achievable. If Santa had a naughty list, he would be on it right now in big, bold neon letters. The two women were surprisingly adventurous.

Regardless of his revelry, a part of him couldn't stop the raw, uneasy sensation stemming straight from his stomach and adding an unhappy heaviness to his chest. Any male experiencing the same symptoms would worry he was suffering from heartburn or nausea, but Clay knew precisely what it was. The strange sensation happened to him last night while one of the girls went down on him, impacting his enjoyment of the experience. It had nothing to do with their skill, sexiness, or openness to engage in all sorts of dirty behavior. It had everything to do with a certain dark-haired femme fatale he couldn't stop thinking about. He was ashamed that he intentionally blindfolded himself. Unable to face the expression in their eyes while they engaged in devilish activities. Activities that ended with him shouting their names in exquisite pleasure if not for mercy. The obstruction of his sight enhanced his experience. Blocking the girls out of his vision and allowing him to focus solely on her- the one woman he would never be able to obtain. Marisole.

He lifted up to sit on the edge of the mattress. What was he doing? He couldn't have fallen so hard and so fast for a woman he barely knew. Still, there was something about Marisole that got to him, hooked its claws into his bare soul, and was unwilling to let go. He texted Joey.

Concert tonight? Are we meeting up later?

He received Joey's response mere seconds later.

Yeah. Marisole's with me. Can't talk.

It was early. She was with Joey? Curiosity got the best of him.

Is she okay?

He stared at Joeys' response.

Yeah. Dinner with Ryan went well.

Clay lunged forward, grasping at his phone, and catching it before it fell straight to the floor. The offer to have lunch with Ryan must've meant dinner, instead. While Clay was busy with the twins, Marisole was being wined and dined by *Mister Loverboy*. Damn it. An odd sensation surrounded his heart. It squeezed slowly until he was forced to draw in a long, deep breath, attempting to inhale enough oxygen to fill his starved lungs. A vibrant image of Marisole happily laughing while taking forkfuls of food into her saucy, tempting, lipstick-stained mouth had Clay gasping for breath. What he wouldn't do to have her perfect lips on his. He shook his head vigorously, jostling out of his brain the confounded idea of them happily together, as a couple.

Get it together, Clay, he told himself. It will never happen.

The more time he spent with her and Joey, the more he realized she was a catch, waiting to be snared by the right fisherman with the gentlest hands.

He rifled his fingers through his hair and growled. He had to maintain focus. Last night was a dream come true- yet- it wasn't Marisole. He groaned loudly. He had to get her out of his head.

The door flung open, and one of his roommates asked if he was okay. He responded in the affirmative. He chuckled into the palm of his hand when the door closed behind the guy. He forgot he had company.

3 ~Marisole~

Lifting her head to glance at her current customer, Marisole stammered through her words as she caught sight of the man next in her line. She took a deep breath, swallowed the sudden dry lump forming in her throat, and continued her ramblings with the female now gawking at her from the other side of the counter. When she cashed her out, she swung her head to find a beautiful set of pearly whites flashing at her.

Clay dropped his merchandise onto the counter. "Hey. How are you doing?"

Marisole shrugged her shoulders. "I'm okay. How are you? I heard about the twins. Must've been one hell of a night." She chuckled under her breath as she zipped the three items across the scanner and dropped them into the awaiting plastic bag. Thank goodness he didn't buy condoms.

"How did you..? Oh... Joey." Clay dropped his head and shook it slightly with a grimace while he pulled out his wallet.

"That'll be thirteen, ninety-five. Will you be paying with cash or card today?"

"Card." He mumbled under his breath while he inserted the card into the end of the reader.

Marisole stared at the register awaiting the receipt to print out after the card's approval. There was a strange, awkward silence that followed. She willed the darn register to print, but the stubborn thing made her wait. She smiled at the next customer while the printer decided what it was going to do next. Finally, she heard the machine sounding. Her right hand hovered over the register while the paper rolled out. Waiting to catch it, tear it and hand it to Clay, yet the seconds ticked by loudly in her mind, driving her nuts like the infamous Chinese water torture until the end of the receipt appeared. Swiping her hand over the plastic bag to release it from the others and handing both the receipt and the bag to Clay with a wide smile, she proceeded to conclude the visit with her usual exit greeting.

"Have a good day."

She turned to the next customer when she heard Clay's voice. "It was really nice seeing you again, Marisole." She stared at him as he shoved the wallet into his back pocket and strolled away. It was only when he turned the corner at the end of the aisle that she realized she hadn't replied.

She zipped a few items across the scanner before she turned to seek out Clay by the exit door. The lines of his solid back and the full curve of his firm, sexy butt caught her attention. She paused from her work to eyeball him until the customer cleared his throat.

"Sorry about that," she said, the embarrassment from being caught coloring her cheeks a bright rosy pink. Clay remained a player; however, no one could deny he was sexy as hell. Maybe that was his secret to wooing women like a champ.

From what Joey mentioned about the twins last night, she figured Clay had a grand time with them. There was no question that the two females spent the night with Clay. Joey watched the slim, tall ladies with scandalously high skirts leave the club arm in arm with Clay, one on either side of him, as they laughed and pawed at his clothes. In a hurry to disrobe him, the three might not have made it to his apartment, after all, or maybe he shared the twins with his roommates. Whatever happened last night, Marisole didn't want to know.

She gritted her teeth at the thought of Clay wrapped up in the arms and thighs of the girls. The vivid visual image caused her to drop the scanner gun so that she had to lean over the counter to retrieve it and zap the few remaining larger items in the customer's cart. Though she had no claim to him, the thought of Clay fondling women in his bed disturbed her. She supposed the idea of having sex with twins was every man's idea of heaven and since Clay was undoubtedly a man... No. She had to give Clay the benefit of the doubt.

Besides, what he did romantically or not was none of her business. It seemed charity work and catering to women's desires were Clay's important pastimes. Only the former involved Marisole, at times, when she was unlucky enough to find him working at one of her events. She couldn't dismiss the fact that her coincidental bumping into him seemed to increase over the past month. Maybe he had always attended the same events, but she never noticed him before? She stifled a laugh at the ridiculousness of her idea. Clay was a looker, and if he had attended her charity events before, she would not have been able to stop herself. She would have noticed him.

Hours later, while seated next to Ryan in the large auditorium, she rolled back her shoulders and found Clay again. This time, she hadn't been looking for him. He was seated next to two people that were definitely female but must not have been the famous twins. Instead, these two women, who looked nothing alike, giggled merrily while they plastered themselves across the arms of his chair, stretching over him and straining out the remaining air between them and Clay. By the way, they acted, they seemed ready to sit in his lap and claim their gifts as if he were Santa Claus ready to reward them.

Sitting in front of Clay were two teen boys who seemed to know him. They laughed as Clay leaned over and said something to them. He then sat back in his seat while they flipped out their cellphones. They brought them up to their faces and stared at them intently, as if a portal would open up within the keypad and send them off to Never, Never Land, the opportunity being one they didn't want to miss. Who were these two? Did she miss the memo declaring Clay had kids?

She turned toward Ryan when he repeated her name. Ryan asked her something, and then he asked again when she didn't respond. She blinked her eyes and tried to make out what he said, but it all sounded like a foreign language at the moment in her fuzzy, clouded thoughts.

"Are you okay?"

"Yes. I guess I got wrapped up in my thoughts. I'm enjoying tonight, Ryan. Thank you." She intertwined her fingers within his when Joey appeared with Paige. Bounding out of her seat, she leaned forward to give Paige a hug.

Paige whispered in her ear, "How's Ryan?"

Marisole smiled. "Good. How's Joey?"

Paige winked. "Hopefully, bad."

Marisole jerked her head to her left. "Clay's here."

"Yeah. Joey said he would be. We're sitting next to him."

"Oh, really?" Marisole peeked over at Clay and found the two horny ladies next to him, gone. She frowned when she looked back at Paige, wondering where they went or if they made plans to meet up with him after the game.

"Who are the guys sitting in front of him? Not his roommates. Right?"

"I don't know." She craned her neck toward Joey. "Hey, love, who are the two with Clay?"

"Oh, the one on the right, in front of him is Leon, his friend from the agency he volunteers with. They work with kids from bad neighborhoods and pair them up with mentors. He's been with Leon for three years, I think. He really likes him. Thinks he's got a lot of potential. He's always talking about him. I don't know who the one is next to Leon. Maybe he brought a friend? "

Marisole stared at Clay as he and the teenagers bantered back and forth, laughing, smiling, and obviously having a good time. A warm sensation rooted in her stomach and steam-rolled through her upper chest, sparking something within her irises and re-focusing the stubborn image she formed of Clay. She knew he engaged in volunteer work, assisting with the construction of homes, cleaning up cemeteries, increasing awareness of local animal shelters, but working one on one with a teenager, directly impacting his life? Wow. It seemed Clay wasn't that bad, after all.

"Do you want to sit next to your friends?" Ryan's question threw her off guard. Did she? No. Sitting next to Clay, no matter how philanthropic he'd become in the last ten minutes, was still a bad idea. At least when it came to the ladies, he remained a wolf in sheep's clothing and, definitely, not trustworthy.

Throughout the event, she realized nothing else changed. Clay didn't notice her. Even during intermission, he never looked her way. She was almost certain Joey mentioned she was in the audience, but he didn't turn his head, once, to investigate or she would've waved at him. Maybe he remained sore at her silence at the store earlier today? His comment to her, in the end, was a bit strange and unexpected. She had no idea how to reply. Was he still interested in being friends with her? They shared a common interest in helping others. Maybe she should make an effort to get to know him.

She snuck glances at him amidst the darkness of the theater as the lights went down. Ryan squeezed her fingers, leaned over and gave her a kiss on the cheek. She turned to him with a surprised smile.

"I really like you."

Her smile widened. "I like you too."

She did. Ryan was fun, warm, and friendly, but then there was Clay. He was hot, caring, and unattainable. Clay was the exact opposite of the man she ultimately searched for. For the life of her, she couldn't figure out why she was drawn to the man and why she couldn't stop thinking about him. He was far from what she envisioned for a potential suitor. She tried to convince herself she wasn't attracted to him, but it was a lie. She was, and it was not something she was proud of. If there was a way to subdue his mojo, she would've brewed up a cauldron full of the stuff to keep her heart and sanity safe. In the meantime, she avoided him whenever she and Joey attended functions with him in tow. Or at least she tried to. Her attempts to escape him were almost always thwarted when Clay casually strolled up to her, making a point of saying something to her. He seemed to always find a way to make his presence known to her except for now.

Marisole's heart dropped when she spotted Clay moving through the departing crowd shortly after the curtains swept the stage, followed by Leon and his friend. She considered accompanying Paige and Joey to the local diner, with Ryan, when she contemplated the long day ahead of her tomorrow. Instead, she and Ryan said their good-bye's outside her dorm room. Ryan dove in for a kiss on the cheek but instead received her lips molded across his. His eyes widened and lit up seconds before he slid his hands down her sides and squeezed her bottom. With a husky tone of voice, she whispered into his ear, "another time," winking at Ryan before she slipped inside her dorm room and closed the door behind her. She slid her bottom to the floor and sighed. What the hell was she doing? Ryan's lingering kiss tingled on her lips. She touched her fingers across the remnants of where he'd been while images of her and Ryan entangled between the sheets intruded. It had been a while since she'd let herself have that type of fun, and Ryan had shown interest. Maybe next time they'd visit the make-out spot off campus, she heard about but never went to, and Ryan would get much more than a kiss.

Two weeks into dating and Marisole was dropping her underwear for a boy, who was a freshman! She couldn't believe it. Ryan's hands were everywhere on her, his lips soon following the blazing trail of his fingers. He moaned her name over and over and sucked air through his gritted teeth when she jerked down his boxers and slipped his length into her mouth. By the girth of him, he wasn't a kid, after all. Thank goodness. She stifled a giggle at her observation and did her best to slide her lips down as far as she could go, but her small mouth couldn't handle all of him, a fact Ryan was not complaining about. Instead, he watched her in between spurts of throwing his head back and groaning. She enjoyed glancing up at him, observing his reaction to what she was doing.

He pushed her away as he got close, switching positions with her. Now it was her turn to lay back, but instead of him using his mouth on her, he used two fingers, caressing them over her sensitive pearl. She didn't want to complain, but what he was doing with her just wasn't the same as what she gave to him. Before she could say anything, he apologized, telling her he couldn't stomach the smell down there.

An invisible blow struck her low in the chest. She frowned, unable to hide her disappointment, yet she didn't want to hurt Ryan by not following through with what they started. Her previous lovers had been generous with her, some more than others, so his refusal to reciprocate, in a sense, had her questioning if they could continue. She didn't want to be selfish, but it was different, and she wasn't sure if she was okay with it. If they were to continue their relationship, however, now was not the time to consider anything beyond her pending orgasm.

Her breath hitched, and her natural rhythm of air in-air out escalated. He stopped before she plunged over the crest and pushed open her thighs. She threw her legs around his waist, encouraging him to continue. Maybe incredible sex with Ryan would make up for the fact that he wouldn't go down on her now or ever. For a fleeting moment, she pondered if Clay went down on the girls he took home? She flicked the thought out of her mind though preventing herself from thinking about Clay proved difficult. The more she told herself to stop thinking of him, the more his image appeared clearly and vividly in her head, reminding her of her senseless attraction to him.

As Ryan scissored in and out of her, murmuring sounds and foreign words that may or may not have been real words, she couldn't help considering where Clay was tonight. Was he with Leon or with another one of his famous one-night stands? Was he with the two girls earlier who couldn't keep their hands off him at the game? Most importantly, why did she care where or who he was with? Especially when Joey warned her about him.

She was with Ryan, and he deserved her focus and concentration, not Clay. She opened her eyes to gaze at Ryan, who hovered over her, staring into her face, beads of sweat glistening across his forehead. It was warm in the car, and the space between them had formed a thin, slick layer of wet that slid their two bodies easily together like well-oiled parts of a machine. She glanced up at the fogged up windows occasionally to make sure there were no faces at the window or worse- cellphones or video cameras. He leaned over and kissed her, bringing her back to the present. She liked him. Ryan was a good man, but she pictured their first time together differently and more intimate.

"Are you okay?' He whispered, pausing to get her reaction.

"Yes." She kissed his chin, moving slowly toward his lips to run her tongue over his pert, closed mouth. When he opened his lips, she took advantage and slipped her tongue through, causing a groan to escape him.

He lifted up for a second before continuing what she started, planting a long row of kisses down her neck. "You taste delicious."

She moaned and closed her eyes as he quickened his pace. He grunted once then twice and fell on top of her, surprising her supple body, and effectively knocking the wind out of her. She puffed air in and out while his entire body lay limp across her until she could get a good grip on his shoulders. Planting the palms of her hands across each rounded shoulder, she pushed as hard as she could but his body didn't budge.

She forced words out that ended in a whisper. "Can't...ca-can't breathe." She gasped when he still didn't move. "Please." She scooted some more. He tumbled sideways, almost rolling off the backseat. Realizing her error, she clawed at him to keep him from falling off the edge as he shouted out loud, losing his grip on her.

"Why did you push me?" He yelled, his face flushed a crimson red. She blinked, surprised his voice became stern.

"I couldn't breathe."

His eyebrows drew together with his grimace. "Why didn't you tell me?"

"I did." There was an unsteady silence as he laid his head across her shoulder. She stared up at the ceiling unsure of what to do next. Was he really that mad at her?

He ran his index finger down the length of her arm. "That was incredible. We should do it again." God. She hoped not. Once was enough and the way he looked at her just then... Before she could protest, his hand shoved between her thighs. She opened her mouth to say something when her traitorous body, lost in the moment, arched her back. His lithe, talented fingers strummed her like a guitar. He wasn't mad at her. He wanted her. She couldn't let him down. Her orgasm built as he took her to the crescendo. She stroked her own fingers through his damp hair, kissed his cheek and acquiesced to his exploration and opened her thighs to him.

***

A knock sounded at the door the next morning.

Paige yelled out as she scrambled for the door handle. "I'll get it." She flung open the door and then slammed it closed again, bringing something large with her in each hand.

Marisole moved toward her. "What is it?" She gasped when she saw the beautiful plants. "Who are they from?"

Paige dropped the plants on the coffee table. "One's for me, from Joey. Aww, how sweet. And the other is from-oh. It's for you." Paige handed her the card.

Marisole glanced over the writing scrolled across it. Her eyebrows furrowed. "Who's it from? Ryan? Oh... No... It's from Clay. How strange. Why would he give me a poinsettia? I can understand Joey giving you one but Clay giving me one?"

Paige shrugged her shoulders, scooped her plant up and strolled toward her room. "I don't know. Maybe they decided to do it together? They are best friends, you know. Joey was probably in a store and Clay decided to buy the other one so Joey didn't have to buy both of them, for us. That was sweet of Clay."

Marisole stared speechless at the plant. Having never received a gift from Clay before, she didn't know what to think. The only question that came to mind was why didn't Ryan buy her the plant, instead? Especially after their tryst last night. Marisole, stop. She chastised herself for her light sarcasm. Last night wasn't all that bad. It was actually fun once she turned her attention to touching and pleasing Ryan, instead of receiving pleasure from him. Still, she had to be honest with herself. From her past experiences, last night wasn't what she expected; however, it was unfair of her to fault Ryan for not living up to her expectations.

She fought with herself last night as she tried to figure out what to do. Now that she knew Ryan couldn't give her what she considered an essential part of intimacy, would she stay with him or move on? She liked the guy but was that enough? Ryan was young yet what he couldn't give her wasn't a result of naivety but a choice.

An unexpected dilemma was posed. Spending time with Ryan was fun but should she continue dating someone that would never lead to anything serious? They were both in college and love was not supposed to be serious, after all- or was it? She grappled with herself until even she was confused about the nature of their relationship and what she needed to do to be fair to him.

She finally came to the probable conclusion the problem stemmed from the fact that it was Ryan. Sure, he was to fun to hang out with and sex with him wasn't stellar but they both enjoyed themselves last night. Despite all the facts projecting themselves in her mind, the best thing to do stood out at her like a sore thumb. They were better off as friends, maybe even friends with benefits if he was interested; however, anything else would be stringing him along and she couldn't do that to the poor guy. She wasn't that type of person.

So when the time came for their next party, Ryan already understood he was newly single but he invited her along anyway. Little did she know Clay would be there, too.

4 ~Clay~

S traightening the cuffs of his suit jacket, he walked into the celebratory event and shut the large glass-encased door behind him. The gathering, being a semi- formal affair only, meant he didn't have to bother with a tie and he had sighed with relief as he picked out his clothes. He never understood the geometric formula for properly looping one, equating the whole sordid business as a sick game of origami he never mastered.

His jaw dropped as he stopped in mid-pace and glanced about the room in awe. The house was a mansion compared to most of the single-family homes in the area. Sporting grand chandeliers overhead, large, inlaid wooden archways and elaborate tray ceilings, he would be happy one day to only own a quarter of the total square footage along with the lavish embellishments decorated throughout the manor. At the minimum, he wanted that luxury for him and his destined wife, whoever that would be. With Marisole around, he considered his future partnership more often than before; trying to picture in his mind what his spouse might look like. That is if he was lucky enough to find a wonderful woman to marry him. Several of his friends remained unintentionally single; the opportunity to find that special someone apparently evading their tireless efforts. Clay hoped that wouldn't happen to him. Eventually, he would like to settle down when the time presented itself.

He rambled through the large foyer and into a crowded space he assumed held the food and entertainment. Ambling closer to the area, he heard musical instruments and turned to his left to find a violinist accompanied by a mini-orchestra. By George, these people had money and they weren't ashamed to flaunt it either. The best part was the owner of the home gifted several charitable organizations with funding throughout the year, including the one he volunteered at. The Holiday Party for the volunteers was an added gesture of generosity this year Clay didn't expect.

A silver-haired gentleman dressed in a suit that cost more than Clay would ever make in his lifetime approached him, his name brand loafers slapping the marble tile floor with each step. Clay smiled broadly with recognition, holding his hand out for the man who happily took it.

"Clay, good to see you. Thank you for your contribution to Aflame Charities. I hear you have been there, three years. It's a good thing, helping those less fortunate. Always remember that."

Clay's heart filled with pride as he shook Mr. Daniels' hand. "Thank you, sir. It is truly a pleasure to work for them and your support means so much to what we do."

"It's no problem. Let me introduce you to my wife, Samantha." Mr. Daniels curved his arm around a beautiful woman next to him in a sparkly dress with a very long slit that ran to mid-calf length. Clay took her hand and planted a kiss upon it.

"A pleasure, Samantha."

"Oh darling, I think you're my new favorite." Samantha drawled with a deliberate wink directed at Mr. Daniels.

"My love, I'm going to have to steal you away from Clay before he makes off with you."

She giggled. "Oh, no chance of that. Clay's about half my age. I couldn't keep up."

"Clay, let me introduce you to the star of our other organization, Helping Hands. Have you met Marisole?"

Clay's heart stopped as soon as Mr. Daniels stepped to one side of him and he found what Mr. Daniel's broad-shouldered, bulky frame hid. Marisole stood there in a stunning, breathtaking, apple red-colored dress that flattered her entire being. The off-shoulder, over the knee-length dress, tempted his irises to explore more of her, starting with the naughty curve of her hip leading to her full, round, delicious bottom. He swallowed hard as he strove to rectify the sudden arid sensation in the back of his throat. Unable to move, he stared long and hard at her until she turned away from her colleagues. She then faced him, stunning and speechless. From this distance he found her eyes widening a bit while his own darted straight to her mouth as she chewed on her lower lip then glanced away, returning her attention to her colleagues. He continued looking at her, his gaze roving down her curvy form, but she never turned back toward him.

After what seemed an eternity, her friends left her side. Clay's legs started to move in her direction before his brain could catch up. He circled around her like a botanist appreciating a rare, unique flower.

"Hello Clay," she offered before he could form intelligible words. "No twins tonight?"

He stopped in front of her, a mischievous smile adorning his face but she shied away. He lifted her chin up with the tip of his index finger and looked straight into her eyes. "It bothers you, doesn't it?"

"I'm sorry. I shouldn't have said anything. My tongue sometimes runs away with me before my mind catches up."

He released her and gave her a wicked grin. "I can imagine your tongue does all sorts of other things, too."

Her eyes widened and her mouth dropped in a loud gasp.

"Finally, I've left you speechless. I don't think you've ever been without a flippant or sarcastic comment around me."

"I'm not that bad."

"No. You're not." Clay followed the trail of a familiar sound behind her and found Ryan, staring back at him. Clay grimaced. "Oh, I see you've brought your chaperone tonight."

"You don't like Ryan, do you?"

"I have my reasons. So does Joey."

"Yes but I don't understand why you have an opinion where I'm concerned. Don't you have other things to attend to like finding your next date?" She slapped a hand over her mouth. "Oh my god, I am so sorry. I don't mean to comment on your love life so freely. It's none of my business."

He chuckled. "It's okay. I like a woman with an opinion, especially when it's not requested." He winked.

"My opinion doesn't matter. I apologize. What you do or don't do isn't my concern. Same as what I do with Ryan."

He leaned in to whisper into her ear. He could've sworn she drew in a deep breath of air and held it that same moment his warm breath caressed her shoulder. "I agree." He lifted up to find Ryan placing a possessive arm across her shoulder. Clay grinned at the maneuver before he dismissed himself from the conversation. "I'll leave you two alone."

Marisole grabbed at his hand as he tried to walk away. "Wait!" Clay's gaze swept over her fingers on top of his before alighting on her face. "I should thank you for the poinsettia plant. It's really beautiful though I don't know why you did it."

"Everyone should have something beautiful for Christmas."

Marisole smiled, shyly. "Thank you. That was very sweet of you."

"You're welcome, Marisole." He swiveled on one foot and made his way to the bar, his concentration switching to acknowledging several of his colleagues along the way.

Ordering a cold brew, he took the glass and slugged back a short swig, reveling in the moments between sips to ponder Marisole. She was a complex, intelligent, fiery female. He remained clueless as to why she was with someone as bland as Ryan. He snuck a glance in her direction to find her and Ryan vanished for some other part of the house, possibly the upstairs bedrooms. A sudden queasiness slammed into his gut with the image of them, in each other's arms with their legs intertwined, forming in his mind. He had no claim on Marisole. He only wanted better for her though he was certain her version of 'better' did not include the likes of him.

Clay was the one-night stand, fun for a weekend type of guy. He wasn't the one you brought home to meet the parents for he never stuck around long enough to build a relationship that would lead to that step. Of course, he'd never met a woman like Marisole before...

He turned toward the familiar voices approaching him and fist-bumped several of his friends as they sat down on barstools next to him. He sighed, grateful for the distraction.

Though Joey volunteered occasionally for Aflame, he wasn't a stalwart like Clay. Clay believed in giving back. When he reached the level of personal success he expected, he would do more by giving monetarily as well. For now, he was satisfied with the work he did. He was always a "people person" and the interactions he had with those benefitting from the little he could do, while attending college, fulfilled his sense of purpose. He imagined it was the same for Marisole. There was just something about helping others and witnessing their grateful smiles that validated one's purpose like nothing else in the world could do.

The homeless had a special place in his heart. Having experienced homelessness, when his alcoholic father took off and left them to pursue a better deal, he and his mother survived in shelter, after shelter until she found one that took an interest in their family and helped her get back on her feet. He was ten years old at the time and he would never forget how much she struggled. She cried at night, muffling her wails into her thin pillow, but he heard them anyway. He swore he would never abandon his family like his dad did. It was tough being the new kid in school but the experience brought them closer than they'd ever been before and for that, he was thankful.

Grabbing his cellphone out of his front pocket, he excused himself and headed outside when he caught Marisole looking his way. Shutting the door behind him, he scrolled through names and then tapped on one of them. He then punched the green button near the bottom of the screen and placed the phone up to his ear.

"Hey, mom. I just wanted to let you know I was thinking about you. I hope everything goes well tonight. Be safe and call me later. I love you."

He looked at his phone as he ended the call. His mom was on a date tonight. It was the first one she'd been on in a long while and Clay was concerned. Now that Clay was off to college, she spent much of her time alone. He wanted her to find someone wonderful to ease her loneliness. A companion with a good sense of humor or at least one that cared for her and treated her well, that's what he wanted for his mom, the one woman whom he loved more than anything in the world. He took in the beautiful night sky around him, waiting for her return call and hoping all was going well with the date when he thought he heard something behind him. He swiveled toward the sound and found a familiar face gazing up at him.

"I didn't mean to eavesdrop but that was really sweet. Does your mom live close by?"

He shook his head. "She lives in Indiana. I try to see her on breaks when I can."

"It must be hard being away from her. Is your dad with her, at least?"

Clay looked at her, his gaze staring straight through her, his focus elsewhere.

Her voice interrupted the brief silence. "I'm sorry. I didn't mean to intrude. You don't have -"

"He's dead... To me, that is."

"Oh. I'm sorry." Her small hand stroked his forearm up and down in a gesture that was meant to reassure him. When she suddenly retrieved her hand with a wide-eyed expression as if she just realized she touched him and she shouldn't be, he held back the urge to grab her hand and hold onto it, forever.

"You don't have to tiptoe around me, Marisole. I want to be your friend."

"I feel so... Strange around you, Clay. It's hard to be your friend." She rolled her eyes and snorted at her comment. "What you must think of me. I just thought you were troubled and that's why I came out here, to see if you were okay. I wasn't stalking you; I promise." She threw her hands up in the air in a gesture of surrender and stepped away from him when he suddenly grabbed her arm.

"Please stay. I like your company."

"I really need to get back to Ryan."

Clay pursed his lips. "Oh. I see. Let me not keep you then." He turned away from her, trying to focus his attention on the gardens a few feet from where he stood and allowing her to make her exit but she didn't leave. Instead, she lingered, motionless for several minutes, the close proximity of her luscious body teasing and tempting him to make a move, to let her know how very much she affected him.

He waited to see what she would do and gave up when he heard her sigh seconds before her heels click-clacked across the tile floor, the sound dissipating in the air as she placed distance between them. A door opened and he knew she was gone. He disliked being rude to her but he had no other choice. She was with Ryan. He couldn't keep her away from her date no matter how much he wanted to. It wasn't what a gentleman would do and with Marisole, he strove to be that for her.

Still, he tried to come up with a way to better their "relationship". Their occasional run-ins were shaky at best though he didn't understand why. It was as if Marisole didn't know how to act around him. She was easy-going with everyone else but with Clay, she seemed hesitant and unsure of herself. He had no earthly clue as to why she would act that way with him. It wasn't as if he was a delicate flower needing special treatment. He was a guy much like Joey and all the other men in the room with her right now. Why couldn't she treat him like one?

Clay opened the door ushering the cold inside air, out, the sudden blast whipping through his mahogany colored thick hair through the open doorway. Avoiding Marisole and Ryan for the duration of the party was not possible. The next best thing was to immerse himself in conversation with his friends, still seated at the bar. He'd partake in the delicious hors d'oeuvre's and maybe find a female to chat with through the next few hours and then go home. He would get through the night. Tomorrow he'd figure out what to do about Marisole.

***

The collaboration of the two charities was not Clay's idea but with only ten days left until Christmas Day it was the best one yet. With the extra manpower available, the two organizations were able to get double the work done in a lesser amount of time. Plus, it allowed extra time around Marisole without him needing to make excuses to be near her. Working in the warehouse of Aflame charities, moving boxes of toys across pallets and into trucks, Clay took brief moments to glance over at Marisole who was currently busy stuffing large boxes full of goods. These boxes would be delivered to local organizations just in time for kids across the four neighboring counties to celebrate the rest of the year.

"Look out below!" Clay hollered as an overstuffed box fell over the pallet being lifted into the air. Clay backed the forklift, lowered the metal arms containing the rest of the boxes and then jumped off the forklift to help the crew stand the bent box upright and keep the contents from suffering further damage. An argument ensued between two of the workers over whose fault it was that the box was not properly taped. Clay shoved his hands between them and shouted, "Listen, it doesn't matter whose fault it was. We have limited time here and we have a lot of work to get done. It's for the kids. Remember that. Now, let's get back to work and salvage these toys. Bring the packing tape and let's get this on the truck."

The two men nodded and returned to the job. Marisole taped up the box when they were finished and one of the men placed the box onto a fresh pallet beside him.

"Thank you," Clay murmured under his breath to Marisole before he stepped back onto the forklift.

"No problem." Marisole shot him a stunning smile which momentarily left him speechless. The sweat beading across her forehead and running down the back of her neck, underneath her short ponytail, did nothing to lessen her beauty. She hauled more boxes in, sweeping the bottoms of the sturdy cardboard along the floor as she walked through the warehouse. She then dumped them all into a heap by her feet, taking up one by one to fold them into recognizable containers before taping the bottoms up and then placing them beside her. As soon as she had four to five ready to fill, she stopped what she was doing to gather a cartful of toys from nearby shelves, returning to the boxes with load, after load, of presents until they were completely filled. Stacking the boxes next to each other, they were lifted by one of the guys and piled only so high before the entire haul was shrink-wrapped and ready to be moved.

The work flowed endlessly for hours with Clay and Dan moving their forklifts expertly through the warehouse, packing the trucks to capacity until there was no more work to do. After the trucks pulled out of their station, to cheers from the volunteer staff as they headed out, the remaining crew turned their attention to packing the non-perishable goods, which would be additions to the dinners the homeless shelters would be serving come Christmas day.

Aflame Charities also kept a fully stocked food pantry on-premises. The staff took turns attending to those who walked through their front doors requesting assistance while the rest of the volunteer staff worked throughout the warehouse. Today, being Marisole's day to work the food pantry, Clay watched her leave the warehouse floor with a tinge of sadness. The distance between them grew with every step she took, the thudding of her sneakers across the floor mirroring the same within his heart. She was leaving. She was leaving him. He should stop her.

Marisole was almost out the door when Clay ran after her, shouting her name.

5 ~Marisole~

Marisole turned toward the familiar voice calling her name. She tilted her head to one side, confused as to what he wanted. "Hi Clay. Did you need something?"

"Thank you for your hard work today."

"Of course. That's what we're here for. To help each other out. I think this idea of Mr. Daniels' was a great idea."

Clay grinned. "Me too."

"Is there anything else? I have to get to the front to help out."

"Yeah. No. Uh. That was it. I just wanted to thank you."

Marisole shared a smile. "Okay. Well. See you later, sometime." Clay was acting strange but maybe he was just that grateful. He didn't need to be. This was what Marisole loved. Her passion lay in helping others in any way she could. The hard work would pay off with the smiles on the faces of those receiving their services. She was happy to be a part of this experience, helping to bring joy to others during Christmas when their holiday might not have been as merry.

He chuckled. "Okay." She gazed at him as he walked away. How strange of Clay to run after her just to thank her but then maybe he was always like that. If so, she could certainly understand how women fell head over heels for him. It was very nice of him to do though a little awkward to receive his praise.

Clay worked hard all afternoon. Breaking up the fight, that could've turned disastrous, was not only necessary but admirable of him to do. She found her heart-stirring with pride when he stepped in between the two burly men and righted the situation that could've grown hostile. As the leader of his group, she expected this take-charge attitude but she couldn't deny the result was utterly sexy.

Making herself at home in one of the smaller case manager offices, it wasn't long before she was notified of a walk-in. She found herself contemplating Clay and what he was up to at that moment while she helped the grey-haired female into the pantry, bagged up the goods she picked out and took them all to her older model station wagon in the parking lot. Before she left, Marisole gave her a warm hug and wished her a happy holiday. It warmed her heart to receive the woman's toothy grin followed by tears and choked up words of gratitude. Upon leaving the parking lot, Marisole opened the door to another customer and repeated the same procedure, this time with a man dressed in a battered coat, shoes that looked a bit too big for him and a floppy knit cap. His gnarled fingers reached out to hers to acknowledge his gratefulness several long seconds after securing his edible treasures within the deep, metal bike basket. She waved to him as he took off, pedaling steadily toward the sidewalk by the main highway, her heart filled to capacity with warmth and good cheer.

As she headed back through the double doors of the lobby, the receptionist, Dee, gave her a smile.

"Nice old man."

Marisole nodded in agreement. "That he was. Are the others done yet? I think we were all heading out to get lunch."

Her smile widened and Marisole could've sworn there was a sudden twinkle in her eye. "Yeah. Clay just came by to see if we were ready. I still feel weird closing up shop."

"It'll be okay. We'll only be gone an hour and we'll place notices on the door while we're away." Marisole pointed to the window beside Dee.

"Okay. Clay said we could ride with him." Her smile shimmered in the overhead fluorescent light while an uncommon radiance beamed from her pearly white teeth.

"Oh?"

Clay stalked through the room, slipping his work gloves into his back pocket. "Hey, are you two ready."

Marisole glanced over at Dee who vigorously nodded her head. Marisole supposed she couldn't back out of a free ride if Dee was going along. She remained silent until Clay sidled up to her and placed his hand on her elbow.

"You got everything?"

His fingers touching her skin shot pleasant tingles of awareness through her taut nerves, straight through to her core. He glanced into her eyes, his mouth partially open, as if her soft skin affected him, too. She stared into his beautiful eyes, unable to move or speak, and captivated by the sparkle of mischief dancing in his irises. Standing this close to him made her giddy and giggly. She felt like a teenager perusing his face, taking a really good look at the defined facets of his chiseled features. Clay was gorgeous. A sculpted Adonis. Any woman would fall for him. His humanitarian side just made the man sweeter.

The sound of a throat clearing in the background shook her awake. She turned to find Dee tapping her foot on the tile floor. Dee tilted her head to one side and asked, "Well, are we going to stand here all day or are we going to go eat? I'm hungry."

They followed Clay out to his truck. Marisole marveled at the humongous four by four with an extended cab. She entertained the idea of owning a truck one day but never actually purchased one as there were too many other, more practical, options to consider. Marisole was already claiming the back seat when Clay opened the passenger door and glanced back at her. The look on his face showed he was expecting her to slide in, next to him. Thankfully, Dee beat her to the car, eliminating all worry of what to do next, when she yelled out, "Shotgun!" and bounced through the open door. With a sigh, Clay slammed the door shut and then did the unexpected. He opened the back door for Marisole and waited as she placed one foot on the runner.

"Thank you. You didn't have to do that." Marisole said, an incredulous look plastered across her face as she slid onto the bucket seat. Why Clay opened the door for her was confusing, especially since he already opened a door for over-eager Dee; however, the gesture was sweet and thoughtful of him. Chivalry was something Marisole never expected from Clay. It was a nice surprise. Still, Marisole couldn't help wondering if this was part of his charm and, essentially, how he got ladies to fall into bed with him. It was definitely a great ice-breaker if nothing else.

Clay remained silent as he drove out to the main highway, following several other cars transporting the rest of the volunteers. Marisole settled into the backseat and closed her eyes. She sniffed the air and picked up Clay's raw, musky scent- an odor Marisole would be happy to encounter on a daily basis. She turned her face into the cloth seat but the smell was not there. It must've been in the air, instead. Images of Clay's strong arms surrounding her shoulders, his lips kissing first, her cheek and then her mouth, intruded. She smiled as the images turned salacious finding them both in the back seat of his car, his hands uncontrollably pawing all over her naked body. She mewed with the vivid images and then flipped her eyelids open, widening them as she caught Clay looking at her in the rearview mirror. When he gave her a sly smile, she shied away, almost sure a definite heat colored her cheeks red.

Dee's endless rambling continued while Clay remained mostly silent, nodding his head or grunting in agreement, when necessary, to keep Dee talking. Marisole closed her eyes again, ignoring the drone of Dee's voice, happy to think of nothing at the moment except her rumbling stomach, which had started up five minutes ago with unhappy gurgles.

Her eyes still closed, Marisole called out from the backseat. "Where are we going?"

Clay answered. "Carson's Deli Shop. You like the place?"

Marisole closed her eyes and settled back into the seat, her muscles suddenly achy, and her nerves jumpy and twinging with the forced rest. "Yeah, it's okay."

She opened her eyes with the sudden clearing of his throat. He peered at her in the rearview mirror and held his phone up in the air. "Unless you want to head somewhere else. I can inform the guys."

"No, it's fine. It's a nice place."

Dee turned to Clay and smiled. "I like it. It's a great choice. You been there before, Clay?"

Marisole closed her eyes again but not before she caught Clay sneak another peek at her. Clay was one fine-looking man and Dee seemed interested. Maybe they'd get together after this. She half-listened while Dee rambled on, scanning through subjects, all in an effort to keep his attention while Clay stayed silent.

Clay's rough sounding voice cut through Dee's chatter. "You okay, Marisole? You're quiet back there."

Marisole stretched her arms beside her and yawned. "I'm sorry I'm not the greatest company right now. I'm just so sleepy. I think all the hard work did me in, for now. Plus I'm hungry." She wriggled her bottom on the seat, flexing her ankles and rolling them to stretch the taut tendons.

"Yeah, I know what you mean. Today's been a long but productive day so far. It's good we all decided to get out for a few hours. We need it. Plus it's a great opportunity to bond with our fellow volunteers."

Dee piped up, batting her eyelashes as she spoke. "I know I like bonding with others."

Clay turned the steering wheel to the left. "Yes. I get the feeling you do." He cleared his throat, pausing for several seconds as if he were reflecting on what he said. Then he spoke, amending his earlier statement. "That's good though."

Marisole watched the interaction between the two and the bantering back and forth that seemed more one-sided, favoring Dee than

Clay. However, Dee, with all her beauty, charisma, and charm couldn't seem to capture or keep Clay's attention, even after they were out of the car and in the restaurant. Marisole had to give Dee an "A" for effort though, for she really tried.

Marisole's eyes widened in surprise when Clay opened her door again, neglecting Dee's closed-door for hers. She glanced at Dee to find her frowning seconds before Marisole thanked Clay and stepped out of the truck. He stuck by Marisole's side, chatting with her as they made their way into the establishment.

"What are you doing for Christmas?" His question, lingering in the air, surprised her.

Marisole swung toward Clay, the action brushing her bottom against a tree limb in the lobby. Hearing something smash to the ground, she swiveled toward the tree when something else fell onto the ground. She then dropped down to a crouch with Clay following shortly afterward. She breathed a sigh of relief as she reached her hand out for the fragile ornament, catching it just in time when Clay's large hand slapped on top of hers.

"Oh!" His large, warm hand covering her smaller one threw her off guard. She twisted her upper body from the sudden surprise, shoving her shoulder against a nearby branch. Her eyes widened when she heard something whoosh by her ear. Clay quickly swept past her and grabbed the shiny object before it hit the floor. He crouched in front of her, both of them staring at each other until they suddenly, burst out laughing. Clay swiped the pretend sweat off his forehead and blew out a breath of air for a dramatic effect. She laughed at his antics before she took the hand he offered and lifted to a stand, murmuring her thanks on the way up. Then they handed their ornaments to the hostess. As Marisole apologized for the unexpected commotion, the hostess placed the ornaments back on the tree and shrugged off the whole experience.

Clay lowered his head and whispered near her ear. "Well... that was interesting."

She teased, "Yeah. Love my coordination?"

He shot her a stellar, toothy smile that nearly disarmed her. Clay's chiseled features, gentle eyes, and natural smile all made him spectacularly handsome; to the point, she forgot he was a wanton womanizer. She found herself picturing what it would be like to be with Clay, kissing his tempting mouth while wrapped in his arms in front of a cozy fire. Then he turned away, breaking the instant connection. Sudden loss replaced her previous easy, comfortable warmth.

"Your table is ready," the hostess offered, sending a sparkly smile in Clay's direction.

Dee grabbed Clay's hand and led him toward the dining area, shouting, "I claim dibs next to you."

"Dibs?" Marisole chuckled under her breath. With Dee sitting next to Clay, he might never get a chance to speak again. Marisole padded over to the table behind everyone else, one foot in front of the other, careful not to barrel into anyone as they paused to take a chair. In no hurry to claim any of the seats, she left her seating arrangement up to chance, planning, instead, what she would order once she had her hands on the menu. First, she'd browse the appetizers for a yummy bowl of hot soup and then maybe look at the lunch specials.

"Marisole!" She heard her name called and then the same voice beckoned, "Marisole, over here." She looked up to find Clay crooking his fingers at her and tapping the empty wooden chair next to him. Did Clay save her a seat? Marisole glanced over at Dee busily leaning over Clay and chatting him up though Clay didn't seem to notice. His gaze fixated on Marisole until she approached him.

Marisole pulled out the chair he indicated. "You didn't have to save me a seat."

Clay leaned over and whispered. "Save me from Dee, please."

Marisole smiled as she caught his wide-eyed puppy dog look. "You mean, you don't like the company?" Clay rolled his eyes and grimaced. He handed her a menu.

"What foods do you like, Mare? Do you mind me calling you that?"

She shook her head. "It's okay. I like just about everything, actually."

He chuckled. "Well, you will definitely find something to eat then. I recommend the hot wings, that's if you like spicy food." He stared at her, an unspoken challenge glistening in his irises.

"I love hot stuff." Marisole's gaze boomeranged up to Clay's wide smile. "I mean, uh..." Oh God! What did she just say out loud? She liked hot stuff! Like Clay? Oh, God! She cleared her throat and tried to clarify her former statement. "I mean to a point. Sometimes they make the wings so hot it's uncomfortable to eat, you know." Oh no. That seemed worse. That was it! She was done talking. She buried her nose in the menu, instead, hoping he wouldn't notice her silence.

Clay tapped the back of her menu. "The wings are on the other page."

"Uh, okay." Damn. There was no getting away with anything with him. Instead, of listening to Dee chatter on and on about hot stuff, obviously trying to gain Clay's attention, he kept looking at Marisole. She could've sworn there was a hint of mischief to his upturned mouth.

She turned her menu and glanced over the selection. Wings were sticky. Not a great choice when trying to impress someone. Besides, she wasn't in the mood for wings. She wanted a burger. "Not a great first-time date food though," she murmured, flipping the menu over and perusing the selection of burgers. She settled on the old-timer, being as close to an original burger as possible with bacon added for taste. Satisfied with her decision, she placed her menu on the table to find Clay smiling at her.

"A date? No one here is on a date, Mare. I think you're safe."

Oh shit! Did she really just say that out loud? She sought out an easy excuse and settled with a bit of humor. "Well Dee might have other ideas," she said, gesturing to the beautiful female on his left.

He snorted. "Dee is not my type."

Holy crap! Marisole took several deep breaths, attempting to relax the rapid beating of her heart. Did he mean...? Was Clay flirting with her? She drew in one more heaping breath of air before she attempted to, casually, enter back into the conversation, "I'm getting a burger. Are you ordering wings?"

He winked. "Well, I may have to reconsider my choice now."

Marisole leaned over and teased. "I don't think Dee cares."

Clay dropped his tone of voice to a whisper. "It's not Dee I'm worried about." He caught her wide-eyed, frantic gaze. How was she going to dig herself out of this one?

6 ~ Clay~

After submitting her order to the server, Marisole dropped her menu and excused herself from the table. Clay swallowed down the lump of disappointment as he watched her disappear through the crowd, aiming for the restroom. Instead of taking the hint, she turned tail and left. Or maybe she didn't get the hint at all? Clay tried subtlety but maybe Marisole was not that type of woman. Would she welcome full-barreled assertiveness? Probably not. Clay only sought a chance with her. He didn't want to scare her. Maybe she wasn't interested.

"You okay?" He asked her as she returned to the table. She nodded in response, ready to dive into the burger placed in front of her. He snuck glances at her as she enjoyed the meal, her eyes closing upon the first bite. She made a small sound of happiness as her teeth clamped onto the meat- a sound he imprinted in his brain for future reference if they were ever in the same room together again.

He tossed a fry into his mouth and asked, "Good?"

Her groan which sounded almost like a low rolling growl stirred something below and left him wanting more.

Suddenly, he felt soft skin caressing his left arm. Turning toward Dee, she lowered her voice and whispered, "Can you pass me the bread, big guy?" She batted her eyelashes at him with a sweet smile. Dee was working all angles to get Clay's attention. If she didn't work at the same company Marisole did, he'd enjoy a brief bit of entertainment between the sheets but Clay didn't believe in mixing business with pleasure. As long as their charitable organizations worked together, he wasn't going to partake in brief interludes with the staff with the exception of Marisole. She was different. But with her, he wasn't interested in a one-night-only deal. Instead, for some strange reason, he was curious about the long term and wanted to see where they would end up. Joey loved her, raved about her and couldn't get enough of her. That was enough to get Clay's attention but now that he met her, he wanted more.

More would have to wait, though, as the Pac-Man machine called silently to him. Clay took one last swig of his drink and lifted to a stand. Striding to a small room off to one side of the restaurant, he took out several wads of bills and fed them to a machine. He then retrieved the coins spitting out from it. Pocketing the majority of the coins, he fed two of them to the arcade machine to his right and assumed the position for war. As the familiar music came over, he handled the joystick like a pro, brushing past a ghost and eating up all the dashes along the way. Flitting in and out of the game's cubby holes, he shot past another ghost with mere seconds to spare, eating the magic blue cube that made them all scatter. He rushed after them, aiming for the other side of the game board, doing the same to that side as he did to the first when the game flipped to another. This time, the ghosts moved with break-neck speed. Clay pulled right then left, edging around corners when he heard a familiar voice behind him. His concentration broken, he watched as his character disintegrated in front of his eyes after being captured by the red ghost named Blinky.

"Oh no! I'm so sorry. I didn't mean to interrupt you. I'll go over there." Marisole pointed to the Centipede arcade machine while Clay nodded in confirmation, his focus now back on the game.

After several more wins and a whole lot more losses, he leveled up to a whopping four before his character disintegrated for the last time. It was a record for him, for in the past he was never able to make it past Level one. He ventured over to Marisole, amusement springing up the corners of his mouth as he gazed upon her. She was hunched over the machine. Her entire body moved with the direction of her joystick, the centipede on the screen darting left to right as her left hand punched the red fire button, non-stop. He chuckled as she squealed, squeaked and grunted, happy to witness the display. He kept his hands still by his side, the itch to explore her eager, active body almost overwhelming his sense of control. There were plenty of other ways he could get her to make noise and he wouldn't mind one bit exploring each and every one of them with her.

"You really get into your games," he said as the arcade machine's screen wound down to twenty seconds left to continue. He handed her a coin. "Here, please continue. I like watching you play." Her hand hesitated over the coin seconds before she took it with grateful thanks and deposited the money into the machine. She hunkered down again and Clay smiled, watching her bottom gyrate and jerk with the movement of the joystick.

Two levels later, she slid her hands down her pants, wiping the sweat off them, and then shook them in the air to release the pent up tension at her wrists. "Boy, that was good. I haven't played Centipede in ages. I didn't even know they had this game room."

"Yeah, I play Pac Man every time I come here."

"Best kept secret. I didn't figure you played."

He chuckled. "Oh? Just a ladies man, then. Those are my only games?"

Marisole dropped her gaze. "I didn't mean that."

"You shouldn't assume things."

"I know."

Clay placed his hand on her shoulder. "Let's get back to the table. I'm sure they are missing us and we need to head back to work, at least for another hour." He escorted her toward the exit where everyone gathered to leave. They proceeded to the car with a happy Dee in tow.

Clay fielded all of Dee's questions regarding where he went after lunch. He then lowered the bomb, as gently as he possible, after she asked for his number. Dee was nice though possibly a little too eager for his tastes. If Clay didn't have his sights on Marisole, he would gladly have warmed Dee's bed for one night of pure, lecherous indulgence but Clay would not lead her on. He never promised more to any of the women he spent time with. Each of them understood the arrangement. If they didn't agree, he moved on.

"Marisole," he called out to her as she strolled toward the main office. "When will I see you again?"

She swiveled to face him and paused, her eyes searching for something within his. "I'll see you at Joey's party on the twenty-second, yes?" The question was more of a statement as it was assumed he would attend, being Joey's best friend.

He nodded. "Sure. I'll see you then." He turned his head when she said something else.

"Hey. Thanks again for the quarter. You know, for the Centipede game. That was a lot of fun."

"No problem." He smiled all the way back to the warehouse. When he reached the double door entrance, another emotion, the opposite of his former elation, hit him hard. A granite heavy wave of disappointment washed through him, weakening his leg muscles and making it hard to walk further. He stalked through the long corridor toward the warehouse doors, putting one foot in front of the other, and resisting the crazy urge to run back to her. In her eyes, he was Joey's best friend and off-limits, as a result. Marisole would never see him in any other way.

Clay's waning smile, plastered across his face, threatened a downward turn but he wouldn't let it drop. He forced the "everything is peachy" smile all the way into the warehouse, determined to keep it there through the rest of the work hour until he got back to his truck. Only then would he be able to process all that occurred during lunch and formulate a strategy to capture Marisole's heart.

The time they spent together in the arcade room was fun but Clay wanted to do more with her than play video games. So much more...

Less than a week later, an opportunity presented itself in the form of a phone call from Joey. Marisole was stranded in the middle of a snowstorm and she needed a way to deliver the coats she promised to a shelter three counties away. According to Joey, she donated items each year to the women's shelter. This year, she thought she could beat the rough weather. Her car had other plans.

Joey, not a proud owner of a vehicle yet, deferred to Clay to help his friend. Clay smiled as he received Marisole's phone number in a text message. Cell service was spotty and her voice wavered in and out over the line, Joey informed him, but she was unharmed, at the moment.

Heading out into the whitewashed darkness, Clay didn't know what to expect. Was she cold? Was she scared? Would she still have cell phone service an hour from now? All he knew was she had to be okay. There was no other option for him.

Not knowing what he was heading into, he brought provisions. A blanket, a heavy coat and a couple of treats just in case she was hungry. He considered a beverage, too, and dismissed all the cold options for a tall thermos of hot chocolate. Hopefully, she wasn't one of the rare few who were allergic to chocolate or didn't like the taste. Most people loved chocolate but not knowing her intimately had its disadvantages.

Clay made a mental note to learn her food and beverage preferences in the near future. He drew in a deep breath and exhaled, calming his taut nerves. Prepared for whatever he'd find in the freezing weather, he pulled on a heavy coat and locked the front door behind him. His thick boots plodded across the gravel driveway toward his truck. Marisole needed him and he was more than happy to oblige because it was Marisole, the one woman who captivated him and held his interest. His breathing mimicked his increasing anxiety as precious minutes ticked by. Running through the apartment, he narrowly missed jagged edges of objects as he made every effort to minimize any further delay. Neglecting to ask Joey one crucial question, he texted Marisole in the hope she'd respond, instead.

> *Marisole this is Clay. Does your car start? Can you keep warm?*

He placed his phone on the cradle in front of him, eying it as he drove, anticipating her response. She was in a rural area off a back road headed to the highway when her car stalled. She was easily an hour away, less if Clay had good luck and didn't hit extreme weather soon. Her response stirred a heavy sense of dread within his gut.

> *I've tried. Car still won't start. Trying to stay warm. Be careful. Bad out there.*

He gripped the steering wheel, closing and opening his long fingers over the cold metal, determination set in his heart. Clay wasn't going to fail her in her time of need.

If she had informed Clay of her plans, he would've taken her straight to the shelter, no questions asked. He believed in helping others, especially during the holidays. A task like driving her to deliver valuable goods to those fallen on hard times would've been a no-brainer but Marisole liked to do things on her own. Clay couldn't blame her for her independent ways. That made her sexy. A beautiful woman with a warm heart and a mind of her own- just the thought tightened his balls and tented his pants. Marisole was a force to be reckoned with. Clay always loved a challenge.

At a stoplight, he turned on the voice activation and talked into the phone. Letters appeared across the screen, in the form of a text to Marisole.

Sit tight. Be right there. Heat's on in my car.

It sure was. The more he pictured Marisole stepping into his truck and then huddling underneath one of the blankets he brought with him, the hotter it got. She would be a tempting morsel less than an arm's length away and easily within his reach. He could grab her and roll her into him for a satisfyingly wet kiss. The image zapped pleasant tingles through him. He sought to tamp down the sensation before it thickened something resting peacefully below. He had no intention of scaring her or coming on strong. Marisole deserved romance, not blatant self-gratification. She deserved dates, affection, and her favorite flowers- tons of them delivered to her by Clay.

As the minutes ticked by, his nerves tensed, the hairs on the back of his arms sparked alive and danced while worry set into his furrowed eyebrows. Was she cold? Joey said she was transporting coats. Hopefully, she draped them all over her luscious body so she could take the chill off.

The clear path before him soon became muddied, first, with flurries then with more solid flakes of snowfall. He barreled his way through it with determination in his heart, thankful he had a four by four truck that could handle it. Scanning the road ahead, he glanced off to his right side, peering through the darkness searching for her, in case she didn't get a chance to make it back to the car but he found nothing out of the ordinary. A curious object with snow-covered windows, to one side, alerted him. He pulled his truck behind the parked vehicle. Though he couldn't see anything inside the chances it was anyone else trapped in a car out in the middle of nowhere were slim. It had to be her.

Grabbing the bulky coat from the back bench, he pulled his own tighter around him and then exited the truck, trudging through the slush that used to be crisp grass until he reached the driver's side door. He knocked on the window and saw something red squirm inside. A long arm swiped across the frosted window. He could barely make out a figure when the door creaked open. Marisole's lovely face jutted out, her naturally pink cheeks now a striking red. Her hands shivered and her body visibly trembled. Her wide-eyed irises looked up at him in the most beautiful look of innocence and vulnerability he'd ever witnessed, promptly stirring his heart and thumping it several beats faster while a sudden urge to grab her and protect her rocketed straight through his tight muscles.

Without another thought, he shoved the door open, pulled her out of the vehicle and admonished her as gently as possible while pulling the wool coat he brought with him firmly around her. Tucking her into the fabric, he shook his head as he gazed over her poorly planned attire. The crazy woman was only lightly layered in a long-sleeved t-shirt and a pull-on sweater. Thank goodness she wore pants though he would've loved to have seen her naked legs poking out from her usual shorts on any other night.

He muttered under his breath as he shuttled her to his truck. "By gods, Marisole, are you nuts? It's colder than the North Pole out here." Helping her into the passenger seat, he placed his hand on the door ready to slam it shut when her voice chattered a request.

"The coats. They're in the back of the car. Please. I need them."

He snapped back a quick reply, allowing his frustration with her disregard of the weather and her safety to get the better of him before he could form a more pleasant answer.

"Yes, you did. You certainly did!" His eyes narrowed as she lowered her own. He regarded her with thinned lips before he softened his reply, "I'll grab them for you. Don't worry." Slamming her door shut, he trekked back to her car, lifting out three heavy trash bags full from the rear seat which he surmised were the coats she referred to. Tossing them into the extended cab of his vehicle, he closed the driver's door behind him, letting a long shiver roll through his spine before settling back into the car's warmth.

Marisole glanced his way before wiggling her fingers over the air vents. "Thanks for picking me up. I appreciate it."

"I couldn't leave you out here on your own. Besides, when Joey asks me for a favor, I'm there for him."

Her teeth chattered. "Thank you." She turned toward him, a sweet smile lighting up her face. He could not pull his gaze away from her warm chocolate brown eyes, even if he wanted to. The longer he stared into the fascinating depth, the more caught he became. His guarded heart melted, swept away with the residual anger he no longer felt toward her. The woman was gorgeous.

"Anything for you, Mare. Are you warm enough?" He pulled on the front of her coat, trying to bring it closer to her body.

"Yes. I can't thank you enough."

"Do you want me to call a tow company? Or did you call one already?"

She bit her bottom lip. "I canceled my roadside assistance last year. It got too costly and I never used the service. It's something I regret now."

"Don't worry. I have the service and I can make a call."

"Clay, no-"

Clay lifted a hand in the air to silence her. "I am making the call. The only thing I want to know is if you'll do what I ask, afterward."

She straightened in the seat. "What do you mean?"

"I don't want you driving your car. I'm going to take you to the shelter so you can drop off your donations and then we'll call the towing company from there. Then I'll bring you back to your car and they'll tow it to an auto shop or where you are staying at, which is Paige's place, am I right?"

"Yes. But that's over one hundred miles away. Do you have that covered in your plan?"

"Did I tell you there was a problem?"

"But-"

He shook his finger at her. "Nah-ah-ah."

"Clay, it's too expensive. Most companies I know don't cover that distance."

"Joey would have my head if I left you stranded out here alone."

She sighed. "You really are too kind. I swear I'll pay you back."

He shook his head. "No need to. Just tell me where the shelter is."

She rattled out the address. He punched the numbers and letters into his phone, placing it back onto the cradle and turning up the volume to help him navigate through the snowstorm.

He sucked in air as her small hand grazed his, effectively stopping his breaths and his heartbeat. Pleasant tingles fired through the finite hairs on the back of his hand and zipped across his skin.

"Thanks again. You're my knight in shining armor or at least in a shiny truck."

He chuckled over her girlish giggles. My lord, could the woman be any more beautiful?

"Are you warm enough?" His concern for her caused him to repeat himself. "I can increase the thermostat."

"No. No. It's like an oven in here. A nice, welcoming oven."

He pulled the truck onto the road. "Let's go then."

After several minutes of silence, his curiosity got the better of him. "Tell me about this charity you donate to each year and why it is so important to you that you risked your life for it this year."

"It's a homeless shelter for women and children." She turned her head toward the window and her voice dropped to nearly a whisper. "They helped my mom and me out during a rough time in our lives. I'll never forget that."

He glanced at her. Marisole looked so small and tiny in the over-sized wool coat he brought, but with her back to him, she looked smaller and more fragile. Clay knew better though. Marisole had the heart of a lion. "So you're giving back. I'm sure they appreciate your contributions. I'm sorry you had a rough time in your childhood. What happened that you ended up in the shelter. If that's okay to ask you?"

"My dad kicked us out."

Marisole's words shocked him. Clay remained silent, unable to come up with anything comforting to her confession.

"It was a rough year. I'll never forget it."

"How old were you?"

"Eleven."

Clay grimaced. Eleven years old and in a homeless shelter. Marisole must have been scared. And all because her dad kicked them out.

"You were in the shelter with your mom for a year? What happened to your dad?"

"I hope the bastard died." She turned toward Clay. "I'm sorry. I didn't mean-"

Clay shook his head. "No need to apologize. I can kind of understand. My dad was a drunk. He left when I was six. We spent many years in homeless shelters until my mom was able to get back on her feet. They helped us with counseling, food and they helped my mom get a job. I am thankful for their support. I believe in homeless shelters. They do a lot of good."

Marisole placed her hand over his. "I'm sorry, Clay. I didn't know."

"But I have to ask you again. Your mom would've been able to go back home if they both owned the home. Did she try?"

Marisole lowered her eyes. Her gaze focused on her hands instead of the view outside the window. "My dad wasn't a good man. He was abusive to both of us. She thought she was better off without him. Turns out she was right. She got a divorce while we were in the shelter."

Clay sighed. "I'm sorry, Mare. I don't mean to bring up bad memories."

She shrugged her shoulders. "It's okay. It's just life, right."

"It's not how life should be. What you're doing is wonderful, Mare. It's a great deed. Not many people have your kindness. I just wish you had been better prepared for the weather to deliver your gifts to them but then, on the other hand, we wouldn't have had this talk so maybe it's a good thing you went out in your pajamas to deliver the coats."

She exclaimed aloud, a smile starting at the corners of her mouth. "My pajamas!"

"You might as well have been wearing nothing else."

"I wore a sweater. I didn't know it was going to turn out to be the storm of the century."

Clay tapped his cell phone. "That's why there's a weather app so you're always prepared."

She teased, "Know it all."

"That's okay. You keep heading out in your underwear. I'll make sure I'm available to rescue you every time."

She laughed. "You are nuts but you are one funny man, Clay Evans!"

"I aim to please."

She chuckled under her breath. "I'm sure you do."

He smiled. "Are you commenting on my dating experiences when I am trying to rescue you and only you?"

"You caught me but you have to admit you left yourself wide open for that one."

He wrinkled his nose. "Yeah, I did, didn't I?"

"But you bring up a good question. Why do you date so many women?" She shook her head as if to undo her words. "I'm sorry. I shouldn't ask you. It's your business what you do."

"No, it's okay. It's a legitimate question. One I really don't have an answer to except I like women." He grinned.

She snorted. Her tone of voice turned serious. "Do you believe in love, Clay? And don't tell me you've loved every woman you dated unless you are Casanova."

Clay threw his head back and laughed. "I am no Casanova, at least none of the ladies I've dated have addressed me as such. Not to my face that is." He winked. "To answer your question, yes, I do believe in love and despite what you might think I am looking for that one special lady. I am monogamous by heart no matter what you may picture." He wagged his finger in front of her with a cursory tsk-tsk sound. "Now those two women were a one-time deal. I'm not ashamed of the experience but that is not my usual, what do you say, repertoire."

She turned away. "That doesn't mean you didn't enjoy it."

He favored her with a toothy grin. "A gentleman doesn't tell."

She mumbled under her breath. "I'm sure gentlemen, would not do a lot of the things you did."

7 ~Marisole~

Marisole's mouth opened before her brain reacted. She apologized to Clay's Cheshire cat-like grin. The thought of him that night with those two women brought a sick taste to her mouth. By the look on his face, he thoroughly enjoyed himself that night. She wanted to wretch. If it wasn't twenty-something degrees out there and windy, Marisole would've opened the car door and marched back to her car, waiting for a miracle to happen instead of riding around the car with a man who did dirty deeds with women and loved it.

He glanced over at her. "If I may ask, what is it about those two women that gets you uptight?"

"It's not the women. It's...it's...It's your life, Clay. You can do what you want. I'm just very conservative, I guess."

"I applaud you, Marisole. Waiting for that one special guy to sweep you off your feet. Saving yourself for-"

"Oh no, I'm not saving myself. I've had plenty of sex." She slapped a hand across her mouth. Oh lord! What did she just say? It had to be the pleasant warmth in the car loosening her lips.

"Ryan and I-"

Clay held a hand up. "What you and Ryan do or did- in fact- what you've done with anyone in the past is your prerogative and something I really don't want to hear about."

How strange. Clay was willing to confess all regarding the tasty twosome but when Marisole was ready to explain she wasn't a virgin by any means, Clay was unwilling to listen. Typical male. Willing to brag but not willing to hear about anyone else's adventures.

The silence in the truck grew almost deafening as the seconds passed by.

Clay broke the silence, "You can talk to me about Ryan. I just don't want to hear the intimate details of your late-night booty calls or early morning rendezvous."

She teased. "How about my afternoon ones?"

He gave her the stink eye. She laughed.

"There isn't much to talk about. He's a good guy."

He, playfully, bumped her shoulder. "Is he the one?"

"I don't know. I'm too young to think of that. Right now I'm just having fun meeting people."

He pointed to himself. "Like Moi?"

"You're the type I'm trying to avoid but fate keeps running us into each other."

"Fate as in Joey?"

"Yeah."

He waved his hand in the air. "Okay. I have a question. If you and I had just met and you didn't have this perception of me being a womanizer, would you date me?"

She took several long seconds that almost seemed minutes to respond. "Well, you're good looking, fun and interesting but no. You're Joey's best friend."

He frowned. "What does that mean?"

"I would never date Joey's best friend."

"Why?"

"Because things could get complicated real fast. It would hurt Joey if things didn't work out and it would be awkward. I would never do that to Joey."

Clay's face suddenly grew solemn. He directed his attention back to the road. Marisole could've sworn he hunched his shoulders a bit more over the steering wheel.

She tilted her head toward him. "Nothing personal. Maybe it's a good thing you do so much dating so you can eventually find that one you're looking for. I hope you find her."

Clay grunted. The rest of the trip was filled with music pouring out of the radio station Clay tuned into. The music interspersed between commercials, weather alerts, and traffic advisories, the latter two subjects which prompted Clay to turn up the volume.

When they finally reached the shelter, she was glad for the reprieve from the abject silence. Clay had not said one word since her personal dating insight. He did; however, offer her hot chocolate and several store-bought treats she eagerly took. Shoving a rice Krispie treat into her mouth, she was ever grateful to him for thinking ahead. Her stomach, unable to remain silent, growled in response to the goody bag he brought with him, sending a satisfied smirk to his face but still no response from his gorgeous lips.

Was he displeased with her and why would he be? She only wanted the best for him. She genuinely wanted him to find someone good, a great match for his ideals, and a possible companion for his future. To know that he went through some of the same things she did with her father brought him closer to her. Clay deserved the best in life.

He parked under the long awning in front of the double doors. She fingered the latch to unlock the car door. "I'll grab the coats."

Clay reached out to her. "No. I'll grab the bags. You get inside where it's warm."

Clay's concern regarding her safety and well-being warmed something inside of her. She nodded, unable to reject his kind request. Throwing open the handle, she ran toward the building, pressing a buzzer on the right side of the doors. A voice came over the speaker as Clay grabbed the last plastic bag and locked his truck. He threw two bags over his shoulder and hefted the other one in his left hand.

She threw her hands out toward the bags and pleaded. "Let me help you."

He shook his head, jutting his chin toward the female voice calling over the intercom system.

"May I help you?"

"Yes, I'm Marisole. I have a delivery for Grace. She knows I'm coming."

"It's freezing out there. Please come in." A buzzer sounded. Marisole pulled on one of the doors and they entered the building.

A friendly face met them at the second set of double doors, inside. An older female with graying hair and glasses tilted across her nose shoved open one of the doors as they approached.

"My stars, Marisole, what made you choose tonight of all nights to come out here?"

Marisole slipped through the entrance and turned to glance back at Clay, waiting at any moment to take a bag from him but he didn't budge. Instead, his well-developed muscles held each with a sturdy grip despite the enormous weight he must be carrying. "Thank you, Grace. I couldn't find another day in my tight schedule and I know you need these."

Grace slid a large object across the front desk toward Marisole. "Let me have you sign the book real quick and here, take these badges." Marisole took the items Grace presented and picked up the pen, printing their names into the ledger.

She had just slapped the visitor badge onto her chest when she heard a familiar sound. Slipping her phone out of her front pant pocket, she read the name across the screen. "It's Joey," she exclaimed, swiping the screen with her thumb. "He's wondering if I'm okay."

"Tell him I kidnapped you and we're now somewhere in Alaska," Clay called over his shoulder. He ran ahead of her following Grace down the hallway and then tossed the three bags into the room Grace opened.

Marisole giggled as her lithe fingers flew across her screen. "Okay." Several seconds later her phone buzzed again. "He says, "It's good to know you're with Clay. Stay safe.""

Clay laughed aloud. "He knows you're with me."

Grace returned down the hallway. "You two have got to be freezing from the weather. Would you like a hot cup of coffee or tea?" They both nodded. "Follow me to the break room." Marisole trudged down the long hallway behind Grace, passing by several offices. She shrugged off Clay's coat and slung it over one arm. "At least your heater's working. My car died on the way over here and poor Clay had to come out and rescue me."

Grace covered her mouth and exclaimed, "Oh! You should've called me. I would've tried to get you help."

"That's okay. He's my knight with a shiny four by four," she giggled, looking up at Clay as she spoke.

He stopped in mid-stride and made an elaborate bow. "I do what I can to rescue damsels in distress." Marisole snorted in response. He pointed at her and teased, "No lip from you."

"Did I say anything?" Marisole teased, rounding the corner into a rectangular shaped room with Clay on her heels.

Grace interrupted their banter. "This is our break room. Please feel free to make yourself a nice cup of hot coffee. We work late hours so the coffee pot is always on. There are tea bags in this drawer and the cups are over here in this cabinet. If you need sugar, it's here." Grace moved about the room, pointing to the various items as she spoke.

Marisole offered her a hug. "Thank you, Grace. We really appreciate your kindness. We will try not to take up too much time or be in your way. Just have to call the tow company before we head back."

Grace smiled. "If you need anything, I'll be down the hallway."

Marisole watched her as she left the room. "She is such a sweetie." She turned toward the coffee pot. "Well, caffeine will keep me up all night so I'll go for some tea. You?" She opened a couple of drawers until she found the tea bags.

He stared at her. "You really are something, you know."

Marisole jerked up. "Huh?"

"You never stop helping others, do you?" He lifted her fingers off the drawer handle. "Sit. I'll get you what you need."

"Seriously? This is not a café."

Clay held onto the drawer and pointed to the chairs behind them, indicating where he expected her to be.

Apparently Clay was not taking no for an answer. She relented, walking over to a nearby seat and slumping into it. A mixture of happy elation fused with frustration swept through her. Clay wanted to spoil her. This fact surprised her but being an independent woman, she couldn't help the nagging feeling that she should be making her own hot tea and not him.

He took out a mixture of tea bags and placed them on the table in front of her. "I found a few decaf. Which one do you want?" She picked one up from the stash and he took it from her. Pouring water into her cup, he asked, "You take sugar?" She shook her head. He grabbed the door handle of the refrigerator. "I think there's milk in here somewhere."

"No. I have it plain."

He lifted his eyebrows. "Really? So do I."

"I guess that's another thing we have in common."

Clay fixed himself a hot cup of tea and brought both beverages to the table. He pulled out his phone, tapping the number to the tow company into it. While Clay spoke with the representative, Marisole glanced over the bulletin board and took several sips from her cup.

"Okay, we're set. We got lucky. Because of the storm, they are backed up but they called in extra help. They'll be there in an hour."

Standing by the bulletin board, she took another sip, relishing the feel of the liquid warmth running down her throat. "Thank you, Clay."

He took several sips before speaking from his side of the table. "Everything okay? What's on your mind?"

She rubbed her thumbs over the outside of the cup and stared into her mug. "Nothing. Just thinking, that's all."

He stood and walked over to her. Extending his hand toward her cup, he asked, "Done?"

She nodded while he grabbed the mug and washed both of them in the sink basin, placing them into the dish rack, afterward.

She sidled up to him while he finished his task, looking over at the near-empty dish rack. "I wish I could do something."

"You've done enough." He wiped his hands across several paper towels, balling them up and throwing them into the garbage. "Come on. Let's go get your car."

She followed him out the door, her glance lowering to his firm bottom, with his swagger. The man truly was handsome and a gentleman, at that. No wonder he was a hit with the ladies.

***

Marisole stretched her arms overhead and yawned. After Clay dropped her off last night, she had just enough energy to open the door to Paige's parents' condo and sneak through it to collapse onto her bed. At some point during the morning, she must've kicked off her shoes and pulled the sheet over her for she found herself half in and half out of the bedsheet, her body sprawled awkwardly across her bed.

A knock sounded at her door followed by a whooshing noise as the door swept in. Marisole sniffed the aroma of coffee and smiled.

Paige dropped the mug onto the table beside her. "Have fun last night?"

Marisole lifted up in the bed, scooting her back toward the headboard. She brought the mug to her face and watched the swirling tendrils of steam curve up from the hot liquid inside with a gleeful smile plastered across her face. "I was stranded."

Paige slumped into the over-stuffed chair next to the bed. "I know. Joey told me. I'm glad you're safe but I do have a question. How come you didn't call Ryan?"

"I don't know him like that. I wouldn't want to bother him."

"But he's your boyfriend, isn't he?"

"I guess. Yeah."

"You don't sound very certain."

"We're just dating."

Paige tilted her head to one side. "Or is it because you wanted Clay to ride out in his big, bad truck to come to get you?"

Marisole lowered her eyes.

"Come on. You can tell me."

"Nooo. Besides Clay has no interest in me."

Paige widened her eyes for effect. "Maybe he'd be interested if you let him know how you felt."

Marisole snorted. "Not possible. Thank you for the coffee, though. It's delicious."

"Avoiding. Okay. Ryan's meeting you at the Christmas party tonight, right?"

"Yeah."

Paige strolled out the door with a backward wave. "Joey and I will see you later then."

Marisole's head fell back onto the pillow. The day before Christmas Eve. Where did all the time go? Unfortunately, she had to work at the market research firm tomorrow night but today she had off from both jobs. She didn't want to think about the long hours she'd be working tomorrow night, on Christmas Eve. It was strange that the market research firm decided to remain open when other businesses in the area closed early. She sighed. National cable networks, apparently, never rested. She needed the extra cash, anyway, so she unwillingly volunteered to work the extra hours. The only thing she looked forward to was the food and the desserts the company was providing for those unlucky few who volunteered their time.

She nestled her head into the palms of her hands while images of Clay intruded. He had her car towed to a local repair shop he trusted, a fact she was grateful for. Finding a trustworthy mechanic, in any town, was akin to finding a gold needle within a haystack. It was a nearly impossible feat but when a person was lucky enough to find one, the smartest thing that a person could do was grab on to them and hold on for dear life. That and count their lucky stars for being so fortunate.

Marisole's last experience with a well-known, well-recognized shop had her mind boggled. To this day she still didn't understand how the manager of the store lied to her, sporting a cheery smile. She did nothing to deserve such treatment. In fact, if nothing else, she tried her best to be as nice as possible, even flirty to get the best discounts. The fact that he lied despite her catching him in the lie had her flabbergasted and untrusting of mechanics, in general. When Clay offered a long-time trustworthy establishment for her vehicle, she jumped on the opportunity, grateful he knew of one.

Just before they went their separate ways last night, he grabbed her hand and startled her. She stared at his fingers across her own until he retracted his arm and cleared his throat. "I'll see you at Joey's tomorrow night?" It was more a statement than a question. She nodded in confirmation and he left, afterward.

So strange. There was no denying the spark of chemistry between them but Clay didn't pursue women like her. He went after models with girlish figures for one night stands. A one-night stand would never do for Marisole. A guy liked Clay deserved more than only one night. He deserved to be savored and enjoyed. She licked her lips in agreement. Oh lord. Where did that come from? From the abyss of her naughty thoughts regarding the impossible Adonis - a gorgeous man she admired but would never end up with.

Yes, she said it. Despite the number of conquests notched into his bedpost, Clay was an incredible male.

Clay volunteered numerous amounts of hours to Aflame, all in an effort to make a difference in the world. He mentored a boy who was likely much better off due to his guidance and care. And to top it all off, without a thought for his own safety, he ran out in the middle of the night to rescue her and her hopeless car from a storm she was unprepared for, not to mention helping her deliver the coats to the homeless shelter which she intended to do, on her own. All in all, Clay wasn't such a bad guy.

If only she had a chance…

8 ~Paige~

A smile widened the corners of her mouth as Paige stepped into the fresh air. She breathed it in with a happy sigh and then pulled her phone out of her pocket and texted Joey. Stepping off the porch step of her parents' condo, she marched up to her bicycle and got on. Though it was her only source of transportation, she loved bicycle rides. There was really no need for a car in her neighborhood as everything was mere blocks away from the condo. It was only when she set foot on campus that the reality she didn't have a car sunk in. Joey didn't have a car, either, but Marisole did. Having a car was a luxury Paige couldn't afford right now, not with all the expenses she already had with college loans and simply surviving day to day.

She glanced over at her phone, nestled in her basket to find Joey's reply text.

Hey babe. I love you too. Can't wait to see you.

What a sweetheart. The fact that she met Joey was kismet, in her opinion.

From her first day in college, Paige had always lived on campus but Marisole had only become her new roommate this past Summer. The stars must've aligned correctly that day Marisole walked into her dorm and introduced herself as Paige's roommate. Granted, Paige only knew her a total of eight months but she trusted her more than she trusted most people she knew. Marisole had a good heart.

When Paige's parents decided to spend Christmas overseas, Paige jumped at the chance to have Marisole move in with her into her parents' too big condo until the dorms re-opened. She knew Marisole was concerned about not having a place to stay during the Holiday break and she wanted to help out, if she could. Marisole had already confided in her about Clay's offer, an invitation that still made Paige's jaw drop. Marisole was reluctantly considering taking him up on his offer as time ran out but Paige knew how uncomfortable it would be for Marisole to stay with him. When the opportunity for a temporary refuge came, Paige knew it was a dream come true for Marisole. She jumped on the chance for both of them to spend the holidays at home, together. Of course, Paige's parents welcomed Paige to accompany them on their travels but Paige had other plans. She wanted to spend the holidays with her new man, Joey. She could travel at any other time of the year.

Paige still remembered the first time she met Joey. It was almost the end of the Summer term when Paige approached Marisole and asked her to be her roommate again. Paige had her share of unhappy to horrible roommates in the past and being paired with Marisole was like having bars of pure gold suddenly dropped into her possession. There was no way she was letting Marisole go without a fight.

Elated with the offer, Marisole readily accepted and they started the Fall term together. That's when Marisole's friend Joey decided to visit her. He was dressed in a long-sleeved t-shirt which accentuated a firm, broad chest over body-hugging jeans that brought out his...um...incredible assets. You know those moments you read about in romance books? The ones where time stands still and the only thing that exists is you and the other person? Well, that moment happened for Paige. It was unexpected and amazing. She always thought it was a myth until it happened to her and it only occurred the moment she saw Joey. She was too young to consider what their future might hold but, at the moment, she couldn't picture it without Joey. It was like he was made for her. That's how Paige felt about Marisole and Clay.

They, too, seemed perfect for each other and might as well have been cut out of the same cookie batter as far as Paige was concerned. There was electrifying energy surrounding them whenever they were together, like two magnets drawn together. This never occurred when they were apart. But they were both too bull-headed and stubborn to realize what was right in front of their nose.

Joey was privy to this magnetism, too. That's why he warned Clay. He knew of Clay's ways with women and the last thing he wanted was for Marisole to become a statistic. Paige didn't want that either. She loved her friend and she never wanted her to experience pain though there had been plenty of times in Marisole's past where she was hurt- badly.

Men could be cruel. That's why Paige was elated to have found Joey, a wonderful man who genuinely cared about her, supported her and above all respected her and her opinion. Marisole hadn't been as fortunate in the past. She had an unlucky streak which some might have called a long line of confusingly bad karma. She met quite a lot of losers along the way. Maybe that's why she was hesitant to dip her toe back into a real relationship and, instead, was playing around with a kid named Ryan- a guy so mismatched for her that Paige could've sworn Marisole picked him out of a loser line-up.

Though Paige wanted better for her friend, she understood why she acted the way she did. Marisole's heart had been put through the wringer and now she didn't trust anyone with it, at least no male except Joey, of course- a man who was as honest and transparent as the day is long. Not even Clay could compete with the likes of Joey.

Though Marisole would never confess her interest, Paige saw the way Marisole looked at Clay. She witnessed how her eyes lit up every time Clay appeared and how Marisole stopped what she was doing when his name was mentioned just to discover what he was up to. Whether she admitted it or not, she liked Clay, and they were a good match.

They believed in the same things, had similar goals and were passionate about helping others. It was only the small inconvenience of Clay's infamous bedding of women that held Marisole back. Maybe it wasn't so minor after all. Marisole had trust issues. The fact that Clay laid with more women than Paige had dates wouldn't help Marisole's position.

Clay was a man-whore, yes, but he was young and a good guy. Some might crudely say he was sowing his oats though Paige believed he hadn't found the right one yet to stop him in his tracks. According to Joey, Clay was a first-class best friend, better than he could have asked for. Clay had no ties to anyone and he liked his life like that. At least that's what he told Joey but Paige got the impression Clay fancied Marisole too. There was an extra twinkle in Clay's eyes, a mischievous sparkle when she was around that wasn't there before. He was also good to Marisole- something Joey didn't expect from him and wasn't sure he wanted in her life, at least not from Clay. Being a sister-like figure to him, Joey would never have picked Clay out for Marisole. Though he trusted Clay with his life, he didn't trust him around Marisole.

Paige rounded the street corner and nodded to a passerby. She shook her head and let the wind ruffle through her hair as she sped down the street toward Joey's. Joey's decision to return back a few days early stirred a flutter of emotions through her heart again. As bummed as he was to leave his parents' home, during the holidays, he was also happy to get back to her. She almost dropped the phone when he told her he was coming home early. They set up a party last minute with a few of their closest friends who remained in town to celebrate the holiday. It couldn't be a better Christmas and now she got to celebrate the New Year with him, too. It would be her first one kissing him at twelve midnight. There was no way to hide the wide grin spreading across her face.

Paige thanked her lucky stars, every day. Joey was an unexpected bonus as a result of knowing Marisole. She couldn't be happier than she was right now.

LAWYER

9 ~Clay~

Clay paced the floor. He was always nervous when he expected something to happen. This time it wasn't something but a someone, namely meeting up with Marisole at the party later tonight. This party was a more intimate setting with fewer than twenty attending. Clay couldn't wait to be by her side again. He counted the hours as they ticked by, picking out his attire for the night and then re-thinking it several times until he gave up, ending with a striped, long-sleeved shirt and navy blue dress pants. He wanted to look nice tonight. Hopefully what he was left with, after going through all of the options in his closet, would do the job.

His goal? To impress Marisole and leave Ryan in the background, cold and single. It was only recently he heard Ryan convinced her to take him back- an act that had Clay gritting his teeth and scheming how he could separate them, forever. However, the fact that Marisole called Joey and not Ryan to come to her aid, that night she was stranded on the road, didn't evade him. He was glad she called Joey. She didn't need Ryan.

A basketball game with Leon this morning didn't distract him to the degree he expected it would. He still had time to contemplate Marisole in between turns at the hoop. Images of her gorgeous smile, her beautiful face and the sweet timbre of her voice all took turns parading through his mind. No other woman affected him the way she did.

"Clay, you're getting soft. What gives?" Leon called out as he took control of the ball. He passed it to Clay who received it with a hard whoomph.

Clay sucked in air and released it with the toss. Leon was right. He wasn't concentrating on the game, instead, he was focused on a certain brown-haired, brown-eyed beauty who, after their last conversation, would never give him the time of day. Clay was dreaming. He knew it. But he couldn't tell his mind to shut off what he found intriguing. Marisole was the very definition of the word. Each time he attempted to re-focus; his thoughts meandered back to "what if." Dreaded uncertainty and insecurity are what those two little words brought up. Though the words "what if" seemed harmless enough, they had the potential to stir up the smallest inner turmoil of angst that could spiral quickly into a catastrophic F-6 tornado.

"Sorry little man. My head's not in the game. Why don't we stop and get some ice cream, instead? What do you say?"

Leon whooped and ran off the court, aiming for the locker rooms. Clay chuckled and shook his head. The best thing he ever did was agree to be a "buddy" to Leon. Since then he had grown close to the boy and eventually met his brothers and mother. They didn't have much but they made the most out of what they had. It reminded him of his mom after his dad left. Life was a struggle but they made it. They had each other and that's all that mattered.

Leon's mother was a single mom. She worked hard and received little relief. Whenever Clay could, he helped out, even if that meant taking Leon for several hours so she could work an extra shift. Clay's roommates became accustomed to the boy, buying him special treats when he came over and leaving the living room free so they could enjoy the T.V. or play a video game, together. Each year, Clay bought Leon's family the fixings for their Thanksgiving and Christmas dinners and this year was no exception. He planned to bring them their yearly gift tonight with an extra one for Leon. Leon had his eye on a remote-controlled drone. Clay didn't understand the fascination with the strange objects but he wasn't one to deny the boy. He couldn't wait to see his face when he opened up the wrapping paper.

Clay considered what might happen after he graduated college. Three more semesters and he would be done with his Bachelor's degree and ready to move on. He knew wherever life took him, he wanted to stay in touch with Leon but whether Leon would reciprocate was up to him.

Several long hours later he stood in front of a decorated door still smiling ear to ear from Leon's surprised look on his face as he unwrapped his new toy. Leon gave him the biggest hug which warmed Clay's insides straight through to his heart. Witnessing the pure joy radiating from Leon's boyish face, when there was so much strife in the world, was the best gift Clay received.

Standing in front of the door to Joey's party, Clay was suddenly not as confident. Beyond the door was the possibility of Marisole, chatting among her friends, enjoying appetizers, or dancing with her incredible super date, Ryan. Clay waited all day to see her but now, his hands turned into clammy messes of trepidation. What if she backed out and didn't show? What if she changed her mind about Ryan and found him to be the best guy in the world for her? Clay had the sudden urge to get back into his truck and drive away. If he walked in to find Marisole making out with Ryan... Just the thought of his lips on hers made Clay's stomach turn. He should be the one with the right and privilege to kiss Marisole not the boy band wannabe. Maybe this was a bad idea, after all. He spun on his heel, grabbing ahold of the wine bottle in his hand before it hit the floor. The door swished open before he could make another move.

"Clay! Hey buddy, come on in. I've been waiting for you." Joey slapped him on the back and grabbed the wine bottle out of his hand. "Thanks for the wine, man."

Exit plan foiled, Clay followed Joey through the door with a slight frown on his face. He plodded through a cacophony of noise, chatter and background music previously masked by the quiet peacefulness outside the home.

Joey raised the wine bottle in the air. "Let me put this in the kitchen. Mingle and make yourself at home." Clay watched his wingman disappear with mixed reservations. Marisole was somewhere around but he wasn't sure if he wanted to find out where she was hiding. He surveyed his immediate area when several familiar faces approached him. Sharing high fives and slaps on the back, he squirmed his way through the sea of faces to one end of the room and found the bar. He swung atop a barstool and greeted the female bartender.

"What'll you have, handsome?"

He winked at her, acknowledging her saucy smile. "A beer, thanks."

"No problem." She poured the contents of the tap into a tall mug. The froth sloshed over the side as she bent over the counter to place the beer in front of him. She lingered back, her heavy bosom resting atop the counter. "Here you go. Will there be anything else."

"No. Thanks a lot." Clay held the mug up in the air as a salute to her before taking a long swig.

"If you need anything, let me know. Anything at all."

He caught her flirty look before he turned away. Clay never had a problem when it came to female interest except for one stubborn girl. He surveyed the room but didn't find her. Maybe she wasn't here yet. As he enjoyed his drink, a slim, striking blonde female wearing a festive red colored shirt and black slacks approached him. She took the barstool next to him, called out her order to the bartender and then swung her legs in his direction to take a good long look at him. She stuck her hand out.

"Hi, I'm Nancy. I don't think I know you."

Well, at least she was being honest. He'd never seen this woman in his life for he'd remember her.

He returned her handshake. "Clay."

"Oh! You're Clay? Joey's mentioned you."

Clay lifted his eyebrows. "Oh yeah?" Joey never mentioned Nancy.

"Yeah. He was trying to chat you up to me. Says you're a good guy."

"Oh?"

"You really are handsome." Nancy laughed. "I hope you don't mind me pointing that out."

He chuckled. "No. That's quite alright. You're not too bad, either."

"Joey thought we'd be compatible. Maybe we are."

"You know Joey, how?"

"We went to high school together."

"Really? What grade?"

"Senior year."

Clay nodded. "I see. That was a rough year for Joey. I missed my buddy. Who knew his dad would move away his last year of school?"

"Yeah, it was tough for him but we became fast friends. He is so funny. I met his girlfriend. She seems nice."

"She is." Clay waived at Paige across the room. She opened her mouth in an "O" and waved back, skirting around a table to let a couple pass by.

Nancy moved closer. "I only knew Joey for a year but I'm so glad we've stayed in contact. You know, true friendship is rare nowadays."

Clay took a quick sip from his mug. "I agree."

"So, what's a handsome man like you doing single? You know there's a lot of girls out there looking for someone like you. There are plenty here tonight." She peered into his eyes, a small smile creeping up on her lips.

He snorted. "Haven't found the right one." He swiveled to his left, slapping the mug onto the counter. When he turned back to her, he could've sworn she was two inches closer.

"You interested in testing Joey's theory out about us? I'm game if you are."

"You don't mince words, do you?"

"I thought you liked that in a woman, Clay. At least that's what I've heard. A straight shooter, you are."

He swallowed the dry lump in his throat. Nancy was coming on strong. While he, generally, enjoyed women like her, he didn't want the attention at the moment with Marisole around.

Nancy placed her hand on Clay's thigh and smiled. "I'm having a lot of fun tonight. What do you say we get out of here afterward?"

Clay's eyebrows shot up. Normally he was the one to make such an offer.

"You know the only other one I've enjoyed meeting tonight is Marisole. Have you met her? Such a cute thing with that boyfriend of hers."

Clay's head shot up. Marisole! Was she here? "Uh, Nancy, we'll have to pause this conversation for now. I'll get back to you." Clay slid off the barstool, causing Nancy's hand to fall off his thigh. She tried reaching for him. He thwarted her attempt by taking a quick sidestep to his right before walking away. Finally. Freedom. He sighed as he straightened his collar, effectively brushing Nancy off him, in his mind. He glanced about the room as he circled it. Marisole was nowhere in sight.

Pausing by the dessert table, he scanned his immediate area again, searching for her familiar face but she was nowhere to be seen. He even looked over the few people dancing in the corner but she wasn't among them. Not finding Ryan either, he wondered where Nancy met Marisole. Did she leave the party already?

He waited, several minutes and was about to give up when he spied her. There she was -the most beautiful woman in the room- a lovely vision in a geometric print dress. Her hair was up, exposing her delicate, soft neck to his marked perusal. The gorgeous beauty suddenly locked eyes with him and started walking toward him.

She greeted him with a wide smile as she approached. "So, checking out the ladies, are we?" she teased.

He returned her smile. "One. Yes."

Marisole turned her head toward the back of the room. "Oh yeah, I saw you talking to that blonde over there at the bar. You got a date with her tonight?"

He frowned. She didn't get the hint. "You don't stop, do you?"

"I'm just teasing you." Her smile dropped. "I hope that's okay. I didn't mean anything by it. You have a reputation, you know."

"I'd rather forget."

She murmured under her breath. "Okay."

Clay grimaced. "Where's captain fantastic?"

A smile quirked up one end of Marisole's luscious, pink-painted mouth. "Captain what?"

"You know, ol' Ryan boy. Where is he? I thought he'd be tailing you like a puppy dog."

She laughed. "He's around. Why? Do you need him?"

Clay pointed to himself. "Who, me? Nooo. Definitely not. There's nothing that boy can offer me."

She gave him an amused smile. "You don't like him. Why? You don't know him."

"I know enough. I know the type. He's a boy looking for entertainment."

"And you're not?"

Paige's voice interrupted them. "Hey, what are you two up to? Have you tried the cheesecake? It's to die for." She grabbed Marisole's arm. "You must try a piece. Clay, I'm stealing her away for a minute. Be right back."

Clay blew out the breath of air he unwittingly held in. Was that their first argument? He wasn't looking for a fight but when Marisole asked his opinion, he couldn't hold back. He didn't expect to upset her with his comments but what he said was all true. Ryan was not the right match for her.

Clay's gaze followed Marisole's departure, admiring the fabric of her dress stretching across her strong shoulders and hugging her marvelous curves all the way down the length of her back. The enticing view gave a slight tease to the recipient but not a full-blown garish display. From what he could tell, Marisole was never purposely suggestive with her choice of clothing. Her modesty enhanced the alluring, seductive female beneath. While Clay had his share of females who blatantly and intentionally flirted with him, Marisole never did. She never intended to portray herself in this manner but her personality naturally drew others to her. Clay decided this was because of her great compassion, her drive to help those in need and her love of humanity. People could tell these natural traits within her that made up her personality and they were drawn to her like bees to honey.

But now Marisole was gone. Just when he thought maybe his last clue seeped through her awareness, Paige whisked her away. Now he would never know if Marisole understood his final hint that he wanted more than basic friendship. She had to know how he felt about her, even if she never gave him a chance and even if Joey wound never condone their dating. Clay couldn't help who he found fascinating and Marisole was definitely at the top of this category.

Clay grabbed a few appetizers and placed them on a plate, making his way back to the dessert table where he eyed slices of red velvet cake he would have to dive into later. While enjoying the music and the background noise of the lively chatter around him, he found Nancy shimmying up to him. She engaged him in small talk, a subject few others, like his buddy Joey, found difficult to do, but he was good at. They found spots open at one end of a long sofa and promptly took their seats. Nancy took advantage of the close proximity to him and huddled a bit too close to Clay. He scooted as far away as possible from her, widening the personal space between them. As he crunched down on a crispy crab

Rangoon appetizer, he was consciously aware of her attention to him. She casually brushed her hand across his arm several times as she continued the conversation.

Nancy had a good sense of humor which kept Clay entertained while her attempts to woo him kept him amused. If only Marisole would pay this much attention to him, he'd eagerly take her up on her offer. Nancy; however, was like most of his dates: a great lay for one long night of wanton pleasure but nothing more. He was certain Nancy would be marvelous in bed. The way the night was going, with no foreseeable change between Marisole and him forthcoming, he might have to invite Nancy back to his place.

Nancy reacted to his sad sigh, placing her hand on his upper arm and looking straight into his eyes. "You okay?"

His desire to eat suddenly gone, he dropped the plate onto a side table and said, "Yeah."

"You want to get out of here?"

He glanced over at Marisole with a heavy weight bearing down upon his heart. She was graceful and beautiful as always, laughing merrily at a joke Joey dispensed. Clay looked away, his hopeful heart dropping out of his chest with a thud.

"Yeah." He wanted to be with Marisole but she would never change her mind about him.

Nancy grabbed his hand and pulled him toward her. She whispered hotly into his ear, "Let's go, lover."

He glanced back at Marisole, desperately searching for a reason to stay behind, with her. She giggled as Ryan grabbed her from behind and rocked her body against his. Clay grimaced at the sight. Ryan pawed at Marisole, planting kisses across one shoulder while his eager hands slid up her torso. His right hand shifted higher when Marisole suddenly slapped it away.

Almost through the archway, Nancy tugged at Clay's arm to continue walking with her but he stopped in his tracks, curious to find out what was transpiring between Ryan and Marisole. Nancy squirmed beside him and issued a verbal protest. When this didn't work, she grabbed ahold of his bottom and squeezed. Clay whipped toward her. "Not now, Nancy." He shoved her hand off his arm.

Marisole screamed, reclaiming Clay's attention. She shouted at Ryan. "No. Stop it!"

Clay rushed to her side. He plunged his arms between them and opened them wide, separating the two while their voices continued to escalate.

Ryan slurred his words, slinging them at Clay as he stumbled forward. "What are you doing? Get your hands off me you jerk."

Clay shoved lightly at Ryan's chest, staggering him backward. "You're drunk."

Ryan slapped the palms of his hands across his chest. "Get off me, man. I'm trying to get to my woman."

Marisole lifted her phone out of her pocket and tapped in numbers. "I'm calling you an Uber, Rye. You need to go home."

"No, I'm fine babe. I just need you. Come on and give me some loving. Right now, babe." He threw his arms out offering her a hug while he wobbled in his stance. His feet traced an endless square on the floor as he tried to remain standing.

Joey stepped up. "Ryan, I think it's time for you to go."

Ryan glared at Joey and shouted. "No!"

"Rye, you need to go. Please. You're not yourself."

"Yesss, I am, girl. Come on and give your man some love. Come on girl. You know I want it. Want it bad from you, babe."

Clay grabbed Ryan's left arm. "We need to go." Clay called over his shoulder to Marisole. "I'll be right back." Ryan tried prying Clay's fingers off his arm as Clay dragged him toward the front door. He yelled expletives at Clay the entire way.

Clay shoved him out the door. "You need to cool down."

Ryan straightened the sleeve of his shirt. "What's wrong with you man? Why don't you leave me alone? You in love with her or something?"

Clay pointed at the house. "She has nothing to do with this. Although you did say something to her back there to disturb her and I'd like to know what that was."

Ryan laughed, holding onto a pillar for support. "My babe's a little hottie. So fine in her dress. Don't you think so? Great in bed, too."

Clay gritted his teeth. He clenched his hands, by his side, forming them into fists. "You'd better stop talking."

"I'm serious man. Her honey is pure gold. And her ass... Man, her ass is fine. Woo-wee." Ryan laughed. "But she won't let me tap that. No sireee. Says it's an outie, not an innie. Bet it's virgin territory and so freaking good too."

Clay grabbed him by the collar and looked Ryan straight in his eyes. "I said you might want to shut up."

"Or what? You gonna hit me?" Ryan whooped. His garish laughter tempted Clay to deck him- a real good one square in the jaw so he'd stop talking. Instead, Clay decided the best response was none, for the man was clearly wasted. He'd regret his decision to overdo it, tomorrow when Marisole reminded him of what he did tonight.

The door swished open and Marisole's lovely face appeared. "Are you two okay?"

Ryan appealed to her. "Babe, just tell the man I didn't mean anything by what I said and let's get back to the party. I don't need a cab. I want to stay with you."

She shook her head. "No. You need to go home and sleep it off. We can talk tomorrow."

"Well fuck you then, cunt. Who do you think you are?"

Marisole's eyes widened and her mouth dropped open. She gawked at him, speechless. Clay fisted his hands but held back on stepping in, looking over at Marisole for the green light to take the nitwit out, for her. Yet Marisole never looked his way.

"Rye..."

"No. You don't get to Rye me. You think you're something, huh? Little miss perfect. Well, you're wrong. You're just another piece of ass, like one of his many women." Ryan pointed at Clay.

Clay moved before his brain caught up. He shoved Ryan back against the pillar. "I told you to shut up."

"Screw you!"

On instinct, Clay pulled his arm back and threw a punch, striking Ryan across his left cheek. Ryan grunted and his face shot to the right. He slumped to the floor, his body sprawling awkwardly atop the pillar's uneven stand.

Marisole screeched aloud and fell to her knees. She tapped Ryan's arm, called out his name and then shot Clay an accusing look. "How could you?"

Clay threw his arms out beside him. "What? Defend you? He was cursing at you."

"He doesn't know what he's saying!"

Clay pointed to Ryan. "Look, I'm not going to let him cuss at you."

Marisole leaned over Ryan's body. She tapped his arm and murmured his name, repeating his name several more times until he suddenly slipped his fingers behind her head and pulled her toward him, crushing her lips to his. She squealed and shoved her arms against his chest, batting at it, trying to separate their bodies to no avail. Clay looked on, ready and willing to pull her off him with a quick tug of her shoulders yet Marisole's words kept him at bay. She didn't want his help. Instead, he considered whether to stick around to discover the final outcome or leave. He opted for the former just in case things escalated to a level where she'd need him. After what seemed an eternity, Marisole found a way to slip underneath his arms. She slapped his face just as a car pulled up to the curb.

Ryan grabbed Marisole and glared at her, a glob of spittle sliding down one side of his mouth. "Listen here, bitch. Nobody slaps me and gets away with it." He turned toward Clay. "Be happy he's here or else..." Marisole twisted her arm out of Ryan's grasp and got up. Ryan shortly followed her, stumbling into the Uber as Marisole screamed at him.

"Or else what Ryan? Or else what?"

He slammed the door without uttering another word. Marisole and Clay watched as the car disappeared down the driveway and into the street, merging into the pitch-black night. Staring into nothingness, they remained speechless several long seconds after the car was no longer in view.

Clay broke the silence with a question to lighten the mood. "So, how was the cheesecake?"

"Huh?"

He gestured back toward the house. "The cheesecake that Paige said was to die for. What did you think?"

Her lips quirked up into an amused smile but then dropped just as quickly. Marisole pointed to where Ryan's car disappeared to. "I'm sorry for how he treated you."

Clay shrugged his shoulders. "It's of no consequence. I was only concerned with how he treated you."

"Ryan was just drunk."

"No one should act like that when they're drunk. I would know."

"But he's not usually like that."

"Drunk or not, he should treat you with respect. You deserve that."

She turned away and sniffled.

Clay reached out to her. He placed a hand on one shoulder and spoke softly, "Hey. I didn't mean..."

She shook her head and shrugged his fingers off. "It's okay. I gotta get back inside."

He called out to her, repeating her name but she didn't stop. She opened the door and slipped through it, hesitating only a few seconds at the threshold when he called her name out a third time before letting it slam closed behind her.

10 ~Marisole~

Marisole's gut wrenched, Clay was right. There was no excuse for how Ryan acted. The painful recognition that Clay knew this from his own experience was difficult for her to bear. Poor Clay must've gone through a lot with his dad. She pictured a little boy at the mercy of his father and only wished she could've been there to defend him.

What Ryan said to her, she never imagined would ever come out of his beautiful lips. Ryan disappointed her tonight. But then all men did at some point, starting with her dad. When Ryan hinted at her need to cut back on calories, that was the last straw, even before he called her those horrible names. She wanted to forgive him but she couldn't. Being drunk was no excuse to verbally abuse anyone. Besides, the sentiment had to come from somewhere nasty and dark, deep inside. So on Christmas Eve, before she changed her mind, she broke it off with him for the second and final time. To say he was angry was putting it mildly. Marisole had never seen this side of him yet she was happy she found out before their relationship progressed.

Joey's phone call; however, was unexpected.

"He is no longer welcome at my house."

"I get it, Joey. I'm sorry." She was. She couldn't apologize enough to Joey who was, currently, chastising her for her poor decision to bring Ryan with her.

"No, you don't. Clay got into a fight because of you."

"What do you want me to do? I'm sorry. Truly, I am. I didn't think Ryan would act like that."

"No more, Marisole."

She stared at her cellphone shortly after Joey ended the call. Why was he acting like that? It wasn't her fault Ryan went crazy. In fact, she got most of the negative backlash. Why was Joey blaming her? Granted Clay was his best friend but to attack her for something she had no control of? Marisole's insides churned and a sour taste moved up the back of her throat. Did Clay blame her too? She scurried to the bathroom, preparing for the inevitable as she flipped the lid up and knelt on the floor but her efforts only ended in dry heaves. She sat back on the tile floor and pondered Joey's words. Next to Joey's, Clay's opinion mattered most to her, though she didn't understand why. She hardly knew the guy.

She was sick to her stomach with the idea that Clay held her liable for what happened between him and Ryan last night. She would never have brought Ryan to the party if she knew he was going to hurl insults at her and smile at the same time. How could Clay think she brought him on purpose to start a fight with him? She already knew Clay didn't like Ryan though she didn't know why until last night. Somehow, Clay was able to view a side of Ryan she never knew existed.

If Clay blamed her, she'd never be able to look him in the eyes again. A wave of nausea passed through her as she replayed the minute by minute details of last night's horror story which ended with Ryan on the floor knocked out. After Ryan shouted at her, Marisole took off, heading for the nearest mall to clear her head and splurge on a mocha Frappuccino. If she was going to survive tonight, she needed to treat herself to something wonderful. Besides, it was almost Christmas. While others were attending church, spending time with family or opening up that one gift out of the several they got, Marisole was spending the evening working. If her mom was still around, she would've traveled to see her. She lowered her eyes, tears springing to life in the corners. Her mom was her best friend. She passed away four years ago.

She sighed heavily, lifting her head up in the air when she approached the counter and ordered the heavenly frozen coffee drink. No, nothing was going to get her down. It was a mind over matter thing and she expected to master this lesson, whatever it was. Unable to hide her emotions any longer, she grabbed the frozen beverage, swiped at the stray tears streaming down her face and then bolted for the exit door.

***

Ten p.m. and she was finally done. After her mini-breakdown in the mall parking lot, she resolved to stop thinking about her woes in order to get through the rest of the night. Between the long script she had to read and the flirtatious receivers of her late-night phone calls made across the USA, she was exhausted and done with the day. It was time for hot cocoa and a warm, fuzzy blanket. Too bad she wasn't at home right now.

She waved good-bye to a fellow co-worker and walked out the exit door, stopping in her tracks when she found a familiar form near her car. She held onto the door frame, grabbing onto it for support when another co-worker literally ran into her on the way out. After turning to apologize to the co-worker, she let the door slam behind her and proceeded hesitantly toward her car.

"What are you doing here?" It was past ten p.m. and a legitimate question of anyone at this hour.

Clay eased forward off the driver's side door. "Making sure you're okay."

"What?" She shook her head, blinking in disbelief at what he said. "You didn't have to do that. I'm fine."

"After last night, I didn't know if Ryan would try to come by and do anything. I wanted to make sure you were safe."

"But it's after ten p.m."

He beamed that radiant toothy smile that always disarmed her. "I'm a night owl."

"But I'm sure you have other things to do and it's chilly out here. How long have you been here?"

He twisted his mouth into a sexy pout and looked up. "Um, for about an hour."

"Clay..."

He pulled a metal thermos from inside his truck. "Hot cocoa?"

She snorted. "How? How did you know?"

"Get in the truck and have a cup with me. I'm not leaving until you do."

She stared at him, amusement sparkling in her eyes. Clay was really something-something wonderful, that is. She opened the passenger side door and slid into the seat. He handed her a red, plastic cup and she giggled. Raising the cup to her eyes, she turned it back and forth in her hands.

"You know that song based on this cup? Too funny."

"Yeah, it is. I have it downloaded."

She laughed. "Nooo. Really? It is a good song, though." She held the cup out to him. He poured in the aromatic, warm, liquid gold.

She held the cup in front of her nose and breathed in, a smile forming across her face. "Aaah."

"With the way you're looking at that hot chocolate, I'm regretting not bringing another thermos now." He held his cup out to her. "Wait. Hold on a minute there. We should say a toast or something. It is Christmas Eve." Clay scanned through channels until he found a station playing Christmas songs. "There you go. Festive entertainment while you enjoy your warm beverage."

"You think of everything."

"I try."

She tilted her head to one side. "What shall we toast to?"

"Friendship."

She lifted her plastic cup and clinked his. "To friendship." He repeated her words and then sipped his beverage.

"Mmm, you sure make a mean hot cocoa, Clay."

He winked. "Why thank you. I had a little help from the hot cocoa box I bought from the grocery store earlier today."

She laughed. "Really Clay? Thank you. This was very nice of you. And you're waiting for me to make sure Ryan didn't show up was...truly kind. Thanks again."

"Oh no, we're not over. I intend to follow you home and make sure he's not there too."

"But I'm sure Paige is waiting up for me... Well, on second thought, she might be at Joey's."

Clay raised his plastic cup and took a swig. "Exactly."

"I'm not sure if I want to be alone in that place."

"You want me to come over?"

Her jaw dropped while her mind mulled over the words she wanted to say. Yes. Yes, I want you to come over. You and that handsome, strong body of yours can lie in my bed and keep me warm all night long. She bit softly down on her lower lip and said what she needed to, instead. "No. I'll be okay."

"You sure?" She nodded in response.

"Okay. You have my number in case of anything."

"Thanks, Clay." Why didn't she say anything? Joey, that's why. She couldn't disappoint him. If she and Clay didn't work out, it would make the situation strangely awkward for all of them.

"Thanks for the hot cocoa." She stepped out of the vehicle.

"I'll follow you home. I'll be right behind you."

She called over her shoulder a quick "okay," before she pressed the key fob to her car and pulled on the door handle.

True to his word, Clay followed her all the way to Paige's parents' condo. When Marisole got out of the car, she rushed over to Clay, still in the truck. There was no way she'd walk up all those stairs and leave him out there in the parking lot, alone, when he took time out of his night to make sure she got home safely.

"You want to come in for a bit?"

Clay looked at her and smiled. He stayed silent for a long while as if he was contemplating his options. When he finally spoke, her heart dropped to her stomach. She really thought he'd give her a chance.

"Nah, I better go home."

She lowered her eyes to the floor. "Oh, okay."

"You have a good night, okay. You have my number just in case of anything."

"Okay." She crossed her arms in front of her, rubbing her hands up and down her arms for warmth.

Clay pointed toward the building in front of them. "Get inside before you catch a cold. It's chilly out here."

She waved at him and mouthed another "thank you" before she ran toward the building, turning back just in time to watch his truck disappear. Maybe she was wrong about Clay. Maybe he wasn't interested in her, after all.

Marching up the stairs, her mouth flopped open when she found a beautiful bouquet waiting for her outside her front door.

"Who are these from?" she murmured, turning the vase left then right to admire the gorgeous blooms. Pulling the rectangular sized card out between the flowers, she almost dropped the card when she spotted Ryan's name. She read the two sentences several more times before she pulled out her key and opened the door.

I'm sorry, sugar bumps. Please forgive me.

Placing the vase onto the kitchen counter, she peered at the card one last time before she dropped the entire gift into the trash. Ryan and Marisole were over. There was no going back.

***

The Christmas and New Year's holidays rushed by too quickly, leaving Marisole with a sigh of regret. With too much to do between work, spending time with friends and getting ready for the spring term, New Year's Eve popped up before she knew it. However, when Clay didn't appear at the New Year's Eve party, Marisole's good cheer dulled. She was looking forward to seeing him again. Sadly, he had taken ill and wasn't expected to show.

She texted him a quick "get well" message while a strange heaviness weighed down upon her heart. Poor Clay. She could just picture him slumped in his bed, alone, and unable to celebrate the New Year with his friends. It was truly no fun being sick.

As soon as January hit, the months flew by faster than she could tear off the calendar pages. It was as if she was in a vortex, unable to escape. Between the occasional parties, working two jobs, the constant study sessions at the local library with Joey and sometimes Paige, Marisole couldn't keep up. Of course, not all of their study sessions were fully attended. Paige, a very touchy-feely type with those she loved, flirted with Joey on numerous occasions under the table. She played footsy with relish, with him, until he ended their session with a big, cheesy grin splashed across his face and then sprinted out the exit door with Paige trying to keep up. There was little question as to what occurred when he, spontaneously, bolted out of his chair, almost knocking it to the ground mere seconds before he grabbed Paige's hand and took off. Marisole chuckled each time it happened, elated that Joey met someone wonderful to spend his time with. He deserved happiness.

With little more than one year left in college, Clay buckled down and was no longer attending parties, making the coincidental run-ins that used to entertain and excite her, null and void. She found herself thinking about Clay a lot, unable to fathom how he was dealing with the time-lapse and strangely missing his company.

Every once in a while, she'd catch Joey texting Clay and she'd add a "Hello" to his meanderings. Clay would offer the same greeting, in return; however, receiving a phone call or text message from Clay was almost impossible. Clay had her number and she couldn't understand why he didn't use it. She considered calling him but after leaving several unanswered text messages, she gave up. Joey said Clay was busy and likely forgot but Marisole couldn't help the nagging feeling that it was something else. Regardless, the last thing she wanted to do was stalk him but it would've been nice to get past the acquaintance stage. Although Clay had mentioned the term friends once, they were more like acquaintances. Friends kept in contact.

When Clay's final year started, Marisole was working more hours at both jobs and filling up her extra time with volunteer projects that kept a smile on her face and a lightness in her steps.

Three weeks into the fall semester, Joey invited her and Paige to a youth basketball game. It was an event aimed to generate business and funds for Aflame Charities, and Marisole was more than happy to attend though she had little interest in sports. She knew enough about the game to know what occurred on the court and the end goal for each team but for charity and the chance to see Clay again, she was all in.

Sauntering into the massive building, she stared for an entire minute or two at a person on the court who looked familiar, trying to figure out if she knew him. Then she walked up to him while he was dribbling a ball. He was leaner in build and taller than she recalled. Had it really been that long since she'd last seen him?

"Leon!" she shouted, waving her hand frantically in the air until he acknowledged her.

He rolled the ball under one arm and stuck out his other, offering his hand for her to shake. "Hey, Ms. Marisole, how you been?"

"I'm good. How have you been? Growing taller, I see?"

He shook his head and grinned. "Yeah, mama tells me all the time that she has more mouths to feed because I take up two now."

"I'm so glad you are doing well." She pointed at his jersey. "So, you're on the team? I didn't know you played."

"Yeah, Clay recruited me. It's a lot of fun plus I've made new friends."

She nodded. "That's good."

"Well, got to get back now."

"You take care, Leon. I'll be watching from the stands."

He flashed her a toothy grin and dribbled the ball onto the court.

Marisole followed his exit, her smile crashing down into a frown when her eyes alighted upon a familiar figure standing in front of the boys seated on the bench. Leon received a pat on the back from the tall, striking male. Her heart dropped into her stomach when Leon pointed toward her. The gorgeous male's eyes followed his gaze, eventually, locking with hers. He then returned his attention back to the group. The sting of Clay's rejection hit her hard, zinging her straight through to her core. She pictured their reunion but she never created this particular scenario in her mind. Trudging up through the aisles, she took the seat next to

Paige, giving her the standard "I'm okay" in response to her question. She settled into her seat, focusing on the placement of her handbag before she looked back out toward the court. The back of Clay's head met her gaze. Throughout the quarters, she glanced over at Clay, curious to catch a glimpse of a tiny hint of interest but he remained focused on the game and his players. Leon was doing a great job, though. He shot several baskets for additional points and most all of them swooped straight through the inside of the rim. Who knew the kid could play? Sporting a gigantic grin on his face, Marisole could tell Clay was proud of him.

It was only after the game she got a chance to talk to Clay when he sauntered over to Joey.

"Good game, Clay. Leon was great. Did you teach him?"

He nodded vigorously, his stellar, wide grin fluttering something inside her heart and weakening her knees. His effect on her was no good. She'd have to do a better job of ignoring him.

She tapped Joey's arm and swiveled toward the exit. "I'll go wait in the car for you guys."

Clay called out. "But wait, aren't we going out for dessert?"

She waved her hand in front of her. "You guys go. I'm tired and I have to wake up early tomorrow."

Joey frowned. "Aw, bummer."

Clay addressed Paige and Joey. "You both can ride in my truck if you like. That way Marisole can head back to campus."

After they clarified transportation arrangements, Marisole waved goodbye to the group and exited the building. She was almost to her car when she heard an unusual noise coming toward her. Heavy footsteps squeaked against the pavement as someone ran up to her. She swiveled toward the person, a bit too quickly, while their sneakers scuffled against the gravel in protest to avoid a collision. Clay's hands, instinctively, went out in front of him before he screeched to a halt.

Marisole's eyes widened. "Is everything okay? What's wrong?"

"I could ask you the same. Are you okay?"

She pointed to the building behind him. "Yeah. You should head back to the others. I'm sure they would love some ice cream. I know Leon would, if he's not lactose intolerant, that is."

Clay snorted. "No. He's not. Why don't you come join us?"

"I told you. I have to wake up early tomorrow."

They stared at each other over an extended, awkward silence.

"How come you didn't answer my texts, Clay?"

His eyebrows crinkled. "Huh?"

"From January. Never mind." She lowered her eyes to the ground. Why did she bother pursuing a friendship with Clay? He didn't care. He'd never regard her the way she regarded him.

"I was...busy." Wow. The same lame excuse Joey gave her. It wasn't worth hanging out in the middle of the dark with him, anymore, hoping for a different outcome.

She thumbed her car. "Listen, I got to go."

"Are you still making the drive to the women's shelter to deliver the coats this year?"

Her ears perked up. "Yeah."

"Let me help you. I can drive you, again. I'm sure it will be snowing by that time plus I'll bring the cocoa." He grinned.

"Okay. Should I text you or call you?"

"Either. I promise to be more diligent about responding this time."

"If not, I'm going without you. I'm not going to wait."

He nodded. "I understand. It's important to you."

She placed her hand on the door handle. "Have fun tonight."

He took several steps back, giving her space to slide into the driver's seat. "See you around."

He watched as she climbed into the car and sped away.

11 ~Marisole~

Paige shouted from the open door, "You got another poinsettia." She shoved the door closed with her elbow and brought in two beautiful red plants, placing them gingerly side by side on the kitchen counter. "What are you doing to keep getting plants from him? Do you have some secret mojo the rest of us need to know about? I mean I'm Joey's girlfriend so yeah, I expect him to send me something for Christmas but you... You don't even talk to Clay, do you?"

Marisole pointed to the plant. "The poinsettia's from Clay?"

"Yeah. Just like last year's." Paige shook her head and walked away, shouting her words down the hallway. "Girrrl, I don't know what you're doing to that man but it's working."

What was she doing? Nothing. The last time she spoke to Clay was after the basketball game when Clay practically rushed her in the parking lot, trying to recruit her for ice cream with their familiar crew of friends. Since then, nothing had transpired between them. For Clay to buy her a gift and send it meant he was thinking of her- that, or he had her on a gift mailing list somewhere and forgot to take her off it.

Their plans to deliver the coats to the shelter remained solid, she assumed, but it had been five months since their last chat so assuming anything at this point was being a bit presumptuous. She did warn him, though, that she was going to the shelter, regardless. The women's shelter held a special place in her heart and she was not failing them due to Clay's non-committal ways.

She fingered a rosy leaf and smiled. Regardless of his intention, it was really sweet of him to have the plant delivered to her. She didn't expect the same gesture as last year which made the surprise gift more special. She picked up the plant and brought it to her bedroom, placing it on the edge of her desk, partially in the shadow of the window blinds. The one from last year stood tall, propped up on the other side of the long window. With her far from green thumbs, she was surprised it lasted an entire year in her company. Definitely this plant was a survivor for Marisole was the worst gardener ever, and now, the beautiful poinsettia, she named Poinsy had a companion. She sat in the rolling office chair, leaned her elbows across the desk and stared at her new plant. It was such a pretty little thing with bright red petals- a surprising but thoughtful gift from Clay. She supposed, after graduation, when she adopted a puppy, she would have to give them away since the floral beauties were deadly to dogs. For now, though, she'd enjoy them as the items they were. Lovely, fun, naturist additions to the serious backdrop of her dorm room.

Sliding her cell phone toward her, she scrolled through the names in her contact list until she reached his. Her finger hovered over Clay's name. She grappled with herself whether to call him or not. The last time she texted him, he didn't respond. Would a phone call be better even at the risk of dead air? She glanced over his name, a mixture of feelings for him welling up within her. Why couldn't things be simple and easy between them like friendship should be?

She lay the phone, face-up, next to her, uncertain as to her decision. Either way, she needed to thank him, even if he didn't receive the message. She picked up the phone and sent a text message to him, instead.

Thanks for the poinsettia. It's lovely.
I hope you are doing well.

There. That was casual enough without going into details about anything in particular. She thanked him and wished him well. If he didn't respond, she did the right thing. She fingered the little leaves of her plant, lifted her arms overhead for a generous stretch and lifted out of the chair when her phone sounded.

Picking up the device, she read his response.

You're welcome. We still on for the women's shelter? When are you going?

She glanced at the calendar and murmured under her breath, "Hm, he remembered. Didn't think he would." Her fingers flew across the screen.

How about Saturday the twentieth?
Are you available?

His response was quicker than she expected.

Yes. What time?
Going a little earlier this year. How is four p.m.?
Sure. Should I pick you up at your dorm?
Yes. Thanks.
See you then.

She dropped into her favorite overstuffed chair, nestled between the window and her bed and sighed. Closing her eyes, she eased the tension out of several of her muscles by increasing the tension and then relaxing them, causing an "Aaah" to flow out of her mouth at random moments. Texting Clay set her on edge though it never did before. She figured it was due to her irrational interest in him and his ambivalence toward her. It was silly, really. She should've given up on the idea of him a year ago but she never had any control over her likes and dislikes. Unfortunately, she liked him a lot.

When the twentieth came and Clay picked her up, she didn't expect he would come bearing gifts for the shelter, too. It was sweet that he added ten coats of his own, all newly purchased at a bargain, he said. The gesture was too kind and unexpected and brought tears to Marisole's eyes.

"Hey," Clay said, sliding across his seat. He reached out and swiped a stray tear before it fell across her cheek. "Everything okay? We haven't even started the trip yet." His warm body leaning over the console gave her a good whiff of his natural manly scent. She closed her eyes and sighed for a moment, relishing the proximity of his body to hers before she opened her eyes and responded. Her eyelashes fluttered open as she caught another whiff of him. Man, oh man, he smelled good.

"Yes. I'm just being silly. I didn't expect you to bring a donation, too. That is very kind of you."

"Anything for the less fortunate. You know me."

She shook her head. "I guess I don't know you that well."

He slammed his door shut. "We're the same, you and me, though you might not think so."

She was beginning to think he was right. She grabbed the thermos between them. Spinning the top off it, she then poured the contents into two cups and handed him one. He thanked her as he took a sip.

She blew into the cup as steam poured off of it. "So, any new women in your life?"

"Just you."

She gasped, her fingers losing hold of the cup for a few seconds before she tightened her grip on it. She cleared her throat and tried to speak but he beat her to it.

"Though technically you're not new. We've known each other for over a year now."

She clarified. "I meant in your love life."

He smiled at her for several long seconds. "Why are you so curious?"

She shrugged her shoulders. "I'm not. Just trying to make conversation."

He cocked an eyebrow. "About women? There are so many other subjects."

"Well, women seem to be a favorite pastime of yours."

He chuckled as he grabbed the steering wheel. "You don't know me well, then. I have many hobbies and likes."

As he turned on the ignition and shifted the truck into drive, Marisole asked, "Why don't you tell me what you want to do after graduation?"

He nodded as he pulled out onto the road. "Now, that's a topic I like to talk about."

Forty-five minutes later, Marisole laughed at a joke Clay dished out. Clay was fun to be with. He had her in stitches at several moments retelling stories of him and Joey she never heard before. The fact that she was having fun with him shouldn't surprise her but it did. Every moment they spent together drew them closer, it seemed.

Clay relayed to her his dreams for the future. With only one more semester till graduation, he had already scoped out several non-profits in the area to find out if they expected any openings to come available. He wanted to start from the ground up and believed in earning his way to the top through hard work and dedication, two traits that seemed to be a rarity in the current, modern times. She liked the ideas he had in mind but preferred more that he wanted to remain in the area, close to the university Joey and she attended. That meant more possibilities that she would run into Clay in the following year past his graduation date and the ability to keep up with him as he started his new career.

The local companies he had in mind were ones she considered herself. She made a mental note of the timeline Clay set for himself to land a job and all he was doing before his final college term in order to achieve his set goal. He was a clever man, pulling this all together before his final day instead of waiting till the last few weeks to create a resume and hit the streets, applying for anything open and available. Clay had an idea what he wanted to earn and he had a budget set up, too. He had made all the phone calls and did the footwork and was now only waiting for his ideal entry-level job to land in his lap. Having worked at Aflame for many years, he already held the interest of several of the organizations he contacted. A few were offering paid internships and one was researching the possibility of carving out a position for him, which was rare for any organization to do; however, Clay's experience was invaluable and the company apparently realized it.

She had to hand it to him. Clay did a great job of padding his resume enough to entice the best companies to take a look at his experience. He had done well and she remarked the same, to him.

Swinging under the large canopy of the shelter, Clay shifted the truck into park and turned toward her. He swiped a stray strand of hair from the side of her face, sliding it behind her ear before she could remark about the inappropriateness of touching her. The back of his hand grazed her cheek, sending tiny zings of pleasure across her sensitive skin. She stared at him, his gesture unexpected but kind.

"You too will have many opportunities, Marisole."

Her eyes widened slightly. Was he referring to himself, as in she would have an opportunity with him? Gods yes. Wait a minute. No. He was referring to her job prospects after graduation.

"You have done great things with Helping Hands and you are a valuable resource to the community. Just look at your work on campus with the women you help. You don't have to help them, you know, but you do because you have a kind heart. Not many can say that."

She grabbed the side of his face and looked into his golden-brown eyes, the flecks in them somehow sparkling the minute her skin touched his. "You are so sweet. Thank you, Clay."

Wrapped up in the tenderness of the moment, she went with what her heart screamed at her to do. She pulled him toward her and kissed him on his cheek, backing away with a startled reaction when she realized what she just did. Her mouth formed into an apology until she saw Clay lean in.

Oh God no. What was she doing? This was no ordinary man. This was Clay: a caring, generous man with impeccable taste who only dated hot, skinny, supermodels. Clay would never look at her the way he did these women. They were acquaintances, maybe friends with time but nothing more. Besides, he was Joey's best friend.

Instead of waiting for his next move, she pulled on the latch, flung open the door and jumped out of the truck, her left boot slipping underneath her as soon as it hit the slick icy gravel below. Grabbing ahold of the truck door, she steadied herself before rounding the vehicle to meet him on his side.

"I'm sorry, I didn't mean to...back there...I mean." She stopped when he didn't acknowledge her.

He pulled open the back door and remained silent, lifting one bag of coats out at a time and handing two of them to her. She placed one hand atop his. He stopped and looked at her.

"Hey, are we okay?"

He nodded, a small smile lifting up the corner of one side of his mouth. "Yup."

He was either a man of few words or her brash maneuver disturbed him enough that he couldn't put into words what bothered him. She wanted to say more, to explain to him her ridiculousness and to apologize to him again and again until he took it and it somehow erased what she did. If she had a time machine, she would go back and stop herself, saying the same words to him with nothing additional. She sighed when he closed the door and ignored her. If he could dismiss the whole situation, she figured she might as well try, too. Bags in hand, she treaded over the gravel, taking care not to slip again, lest he come and save her and make for another awkward moment. She re-focused her thoughts on the task at hand and made her way to the front door.

All went well with Grace, who was surprised to see Clay again but thankful that the weather was more forgiving for their reunion. This time, Grace received two hugs upon their departure- Clay adding one of his own. When they got back to her dorm, Clay gave Marisole a warm hug and asked her to come to his graduation. Joey would be there, he said. He wanted her there, too. She thanked him for the invite and pondered what to get him. Would Paige attend, too? It was likely since Joey and Paige were inseparable like Fettuccini and Alfredo. One just wasn't the same without the other.

Clay handed her something, dropping it into her hands before he departed. She gazed down to find a pack of sour gummy bears. It was one of her favorite snacks. How thoughtful of him. She flagged him down as he was leaving.

"But I didn't get you anything," she protested, as he slid behind the steering wheel.

"Yeah, you did." He touched his cheek and grinned.

"Well, if you consider that a gift, I'm glad. You have a good soul, Clay."

He placed his gloved hand over hers and leaned over the edge of the windowsill. "So do you. I expect to see you at graduation, okay. I will send you the invite. "

She nodded. "Okay. Oh, and Clay, Merry Christmas if I don't see you."

"Merry Christmas, Marisole." He let go of her hand.

She waved to him as he sped away.

***

The months since that day flew by faster than she could blink. She met Clay a couple of times in the spring term at volunteer projects and a few times as he took off with Joey but spending time with him and being in his company, never happened again. However, today was a special day. It marked Clay's graduation and the day she quit her second job. It was a difficult decision for her to make but with her own graduation day approaching she had to let go of one of her jobs in order to concentrate on her studies. Although the marketing job paid more, the retail job gave her more hours. As much as she'd rather be at the marketing job, she needed the retail job's flexible hours and days to work around her school schedule so she let the marketing job go.

One more year of school and then she and Joey would receive their degrees. It was surprising to think they'd come this far and only had so much more to go. One year would fly by quickly. If she doubted that, she only had to look back at this past year and tall, handsome Clay with his cap and gown. Clay was one of the fortunate few, landing a great entry-level job with a non-profit in the city. However non-profit did not mean millionaire. Clay had some lean times ahead of him as he moved out of the apartment he shared with the guys into his own, income-restricted one bedroom. Joey checked out the apartment before Clay signed the lease and gave it two thumbs up. Clay had done well.

Clay had bills of his own and a student loan to contend with. When it came to what gift to buy him, Marisole could think of nothing better. A grocery store gift card seemed the best present to give someone just starting off. Clay would need the extra funds to help him get settled.

As she listened to the President of the college and the speeches that followed, she reflected upon her last year, considering how she and Joey would fare walking across the stage for their first and final time. It would be a highlight in their lives, walking across campus for the very last time and spending that final night in their dorm rooms before receiving the valuable embossed parchment and the reason they studied hard the past four years. She wondered if Clay felt the same, right now.

"Clayton Benjamin Evans."

His name booming in her ears woke her from her daydream. She stretched her neck up to see Clay, standing strong and tall, with a wide grin decorating his gorgeous lips. He strolled across the stage, shook the president's hand and retrieved the rectangle-shaped, padded folder that would soon hold his degree. Marisole stood as pride for him and his accomplishments welled up within her heart. She whistled in the air and clapped for him, happy to be honored to celebrate this great moment in his life. Despite his womanizing ways, Clay had worked hard, graduating with honors and a 3.7 GPA. It was a stellar accomplishment worthy of praise.

Clay waved toward them and then gave an air kiss to a nicely dressed female near the front of the stage. The lean woman stood, kissing both palms of her hands and presenting them to him, mimicking his affectionate maneuver. She swiped at her eyes and then took her seat.

Marisole whispered in Paige's ear. "Who's that?"

"Joey said that's Clay's mom, Judy."

Marisole gazed over the female and stood back in awe. Clay mentioned her only a few times; however, each time he did, something in his eyes sparkled. Marisole would finally get to meet the woman who raised him, single-handedly on her own. According to Joey, she meant the world to Clay but Marisole didn't need to hear that from Joey. She already knew this fact by watching Clay's actions. Clay ran off the stage and dipped low to hug his mom, giving her a peck on the cheek before returning to the line to stand with his class.

Observing Clay's interactions with his mom touched her heart especially since her own mom- her best friend- was no longer with her. She missed bantering back and forth with her mom, sharing quips and stories and spending time with her but the main two things she missed most about her mom? Hugging and kissing her. She never knew how much it would hurt, not being able to do that with the one woman who meant most to her in the world, until she was gone. Tears sprang to her eyes. She batted them back knowing today was Clay's day, a day of celebration, not one for grief over her own personal loss.

Marisole was proud of Clay. He had a bright future ahead of him. When everyone lined up after graduation to give him a hug along with their congratulations, she stood with the others, smiling at Clay. Once he glanced her way, she came closer to him and then, finally, it was her turn.

He graced her with the biggest smile and held his arms out to her. "I made it."

"You did. I'm so happy for you and for your next step toward your future."

He suddenly pulled back from the hug, before she could give him his gift, and tugged on the arm of the gracious female next to him. "Marisole, there is someone I want you to meet. This is my mom, Judy."

She stuck her hand out and was welcomed by a small, warm hand and a gentle smile. "So, you're Marisole? So good to meet you."

"It's nice to meet you too, Judy. Clay talks about you a lot and it's always great to hear his stories.

Judy gently pinched his cheek and looked up at him, fondly, with a noticeable twinkle ino her eyes. "He's my boy, no matter how old he gets I am so proud of him."

Marisole nodded. "Aww. Clay is a good man." Clay's head whipped toward Marisole. He gazed at her for several seconds too long.

Marisole took the opportunity to slip the small gift box to Clay with an additional card, into his hand. "Clay, I hope this gift will help you get started on your new journey."

"You didn't have to do that. Just being here to celebrate with me is...nice."

"I wanted to. Getting started out on your own is hard."

"What is it?" He popped open the box and smiled. "Wow. Thanks. This will come in handy." He turned to show his mom the gift card seconds before he gave Marisole another hug. "Thank you. You are coming with us to celebrate, right?"

"Well, I was-"

He lowered his chin and looked into her eyes. "Mare, I want you with us, please." The sincerity she found in his eyes and the seriousness behind his words made her re-think her plans.

"Okay, I can go with you guys."

"Good." He patted her on the back with a grateful smile and then turned to another in line waiting to offer him their congratulations.

She had not expected to hang out with Clay, after the graduation ceremony because she wasn't officially invited. Separate invitations went out for the graduation ceremony and the after-party, which was only sent to a few select friends, one of them being Joey. But hers? She didn't receive one nor did she expect one, so when he invited her...

Several squeals interrupted her thoughts. A few girls flung their arms across his shoulders, some wearing graduation caps, and some not. Gifts were shoved at him, which he placed into a large bag by his mother's feet. The women gathered around clung to him, many whispering things into his ear which caused him to grin. Their attempts to gain more of his attention were soon foiled by a few males heading his way.

Clay hugged several more friends and then announced to the small crowd gathered around him. "Okay, I got to take my mom back to her hotel." He tugged up the bag of presents he received. "Thank you so much for your generosity. I can't tell you how much each of you means to me." Marisole followed the group disbursing, taking notice that one of the young females slid next to him into his truck before they took off.

As she opened her car door, she wished she hadn't said yes to the party. If only she could head back, instead, to her comfy chair and blanket, calling her to come home. She would be more at ease there but then, again, it was Clay's day and how many more times would she see him past today? Though he didn't seem lacking in company, she resigned herself to spend a few hours in the café, to show her support.

The after-party didn't fare as well as Marisole hoped. If she knew she'd be a witness to his entourage of female fans, she would've stayed home, instead, wrapped up in a good mystery book but here she was, at one end of a very long table and nowhere near Clay. Having never been a social butterfly, she attempted to chat with those around her but it wasn't the same as being warm and comfortable with good friends. Clay was surrounded by beautiful women at the end of the table, one not being his mom. The one chance Marisole had to speak with Clay, on his way to the restroom, he mentioned he would celebrate with his mom, later that night. If only she could be there, instead. Large crowds never suited her unless she was working for a charitable cause.

Clay spent most of his time and attention with those near him. Maybe if she snuck out, he wouldn't notice her absence. She could be back at Paige's before he had the chance to blink his eyes.

Paige's parents, ardent world travelers, were gone again on another vacation and Marisole and Paige found themselves sharing their place until their dorms opened back up. Thank goodness for her parents who never seemed to be home and always on vacation. Paige wasn't here with her for the after-party, having not been invited either, though she could've come because of Joey, but, like Marisole, she preferred the coziness of home to large parties with strangers. That's where Marisole, ultimately, wanted to be – curled up with a good book with Paige to chat with.

Joey tapped her on the shoulder. "Hey, there's an empty seat next to me. You want it?"

"Nah. Thanks, though. I was thinking of heading back and joining Paige."

"Oh. Okay. Tell her I'll see her, later, then."

Joey walked over to the head of the table to join the others while Marisole checked to make sure Clay was not glancing her way. During the hour she'd been here, he looked at her once and that was only because the guy next to her said something aloud and pointed in her direction. There was no reason for him to stare her down now; however, Marisole was the type of person that never got away with anything so she left nothing up to chance. She grabbed ahold of her credit card from her purse and slid back the wooden chair as gingerly and noiselessly as possible, which was easier to do than she thought, over the loud chatter of his friends. She peeked over her shoulder at him and then made a break for it, proceeding on her tiptoes vs. clacking her noisy heels across the wooden floor and vying for the checkout counter as quickly as she could make it.

As soon as she got to the stand, she inquired with the hostess. "I'm at the table with the big crowd back there. Can I settle my bill?"

"Sure. Let me get your server," the hostess said before she stepped away.

The longest minute ever passed by before the server came back to attend to her. In the meantime, her heartbeat raced like a trick-performing mare in an arena filled with paying customers. She snuck a peek back at the table and noticed Clay engaged in conversation. Good. She might be able to make her escape, after all.

As she added the tip and signed the receipt, she heard a gruff voice behind her. It was Clay. Damn. She almost made it.

"Are you leaving?"

She slipped her copy of the receipt into her purse, grabbed her keys and spun around to face him.

"Yes. It's been fun but I have to go. Please tell your mom I was happy to meet her and I wish her safe travels when she does go back home."

"Thank you. I will let her know but why are you leaving? School's out and summer term has not started yet."

She shook her head. "Uh..." She had no explanation except that she was uncomfortable sitting by herself with no one to converse with, at least that's how she felt the last hour. There was only so much food and alcohol one could consume to fill the time.

"Will I see you, again?"

"Um, I'm sure we'll run into each other. I mean, we have Joey in common and our volunteer hours, that is, unless you are giving up your volunteer work."

"Not a chance."

"Good, then, I'll probably see you around."

"Plus you have my number. Keep in touch."

"You too," she offered, though her heart wasn't in it. Did she really want to keep in touch with Clay, the one that got away? Being near him still caused all sorts of pleasurable tingles to zip sensually across her skin. The man was gorgeous. No one could deny that fact.

He offered her a hug and she took it, though she should've run out the door instead of choosing his strong, warm embrace. She closed her eyes and melted into his hug, allowing his manly musk to wash over her while viewing images, in her mind, of the two of them embracing elsewhere. Instead of standing by the checkout counter, they were on a sunny, remote island underneath a large palm tree, in the middle of a bustling street in Paris or on a white sandy beach in Clearwater, Florida. Either of the two places would suit her fine. As if he knew this could be the last time he saw her, he tightened his hold on her seconds before he, reluctantly, let her go. He caressed his fingers down the side of one cheek and spoke. "It's been really nice knowing you, Marisole. Please don't be a stranger."

She smiled, nodded, and then walked out the door.

12 ~Clay~

Five months passed with no word from Marisole. After they parted, he didn't expect she would text him, not unless he texted, first. She was a traditional female, in the sense, and was not one to take the first step, at least not at the beginning. He understood this and accepted it, yet, somehow, the fact that she didn't call or text him still hit him hard in the gut.

Despite his new life and the availability of a different female population, he still liked her and thought about her, often. At several times he found himself picking up the phone and glancing down at her name, his fingers hovering over the keyboard, ready to text a message to her. Instead of following through, he dropped the phone, every time, and groaned; wishing things were different between them.

During his visits with Joey, he casually asked about her. Whether Joey knew or not that he had an interest in her was unknown. Clay was only interested in Marisole knowing of his marked interest. He gazed at her picture on his phone. He took the profile picture of her the last time they delivered coats to the women's shelter. In the picture, she was waiting for her hot beverage to cool down. She had rested her head in her hands and had a faraway look in her eyes which captivated him and rendered him speechless. He knew he had to capture the moment so he snuck his phone out and snapped the picture, undetected, when a worker suddenly walked into the room. Still, it was perfect timing, for she was unaware he did anything. Since then, he had stared at her image countless times throughout the last five months, wondering what she was up to and pondering what he could do to keep her in his life.

The times he held the phone in one hand, gazing lovingly at her image while he took himself in his other hand, he would never admit to her. To this day, he didn't understand why she left the after-party early. He imagined it was the female attention he was receiving and the crowd of strangers that didn't know her. He had received several invitations that night to warm beds but he had a date with Judy and was not reneging on the opportunity to spend time with his mom.

However, after he moved in, he took many of the women up on their offers. But then several weeks into his first month, he quit, deciding it wasn't worth it to bed several women when he only wanted one.

He lifted the phone in front of him and his fingers flew over the keyboard. He looked at what he wrote and deleted more than half of it. He couldn't tell her all that. He would scare her away. He left one line remaining and pressed send.

Hey. How have you been?

The words were subtle and casual, traits he wanted to emulate when he was in her presence. Yet when she was around, he was anything but those two words; instead his hands itched to wander all over the gorgeous treasure map that was her body and his lips urged him to do the same.

When he didn't receive a response, he picked up the phone and called her. It went straight to voicemail.

Was she busy or ignoring his calls? He anticipated the former for nothing had happened to prompt their falling out. He awaited her response as he immersed himself in his job duties. When she finally called him, he breathed out a sigh of relief.

He pressed the green button and murmured into his phone, "Hold on a minute." Walking quickly past his cubicle, he strode down the long hallway to a set of restrooms toward the back of the building and stepped off to one side of the doors.

His heart surged with excitement as he picked up the phone and placed it next to his ear. "Hey Mare, so glad you called me back."

The soft tone of her voice was heaven to his ears. "Hi Clay. How have you been?"

"I'm good, Mare. I miss you." A long silence ensued.

"I miss you too."

Really? She could've picked up the phone at any time. Instead of focusing on the painful fact of her absence, he decided to remain positive. "Are you free for lunch or dinner, tomorrow?"

"Um, yeah, lunch sounds good. I have a long break between classes."

Several lines from a movie he watched in the past floated across his mind. He was reminded of the friend zone and how lunch is not okay. Still, it was an opportunity to spend time with her and it was better than nothing. "Okay, then. Tomorrow, I'll meet you on campus, at noon at Fox Deli, how does that sound?"

"Sure. Sounds great."

"See you then." He ended the call with a wide smile plastered to his face. When it came to Marisole, he was a goner...

The next day, he ran across campus, conscious of the minutes ticking past twelve noon. He had taken the rest of the day off, knowing he would never have the ability to concentrate after having lunch with the woman of his dreams. As much as he tried to get off work on time, he never did, there seeming to always be something last minute someone wanted him to do and today, he regretted his inability to meet her at the proposed time. If it was anyone else, it wouldn't have bothered him, but this was

Marisole and after so much time apart, he wanted to make a good impression on her.

He skidded to a stop in front of the doors and took a deep breath, willing his rapid heartbeat to normalize. Running several fingers through his wind-swept hair, he glanced into one of the long panes of glass at the front of the café and spotted her inside. He waved at her and smiled, his heartbeat threatening to rev back up with the added awareness of her presence. He pulled open the door and stepped inside. She surprised him with a hug. He held her longer than was expected unwilling to let her go as quickly as normal protocol would have instructed.

"Clay, you act like you haven't seen me in years," she teased. If she only knew the five months apart seemed like years, already.

"Oh, I forgot," he exclaimed, pulling a small bag out from his front jean pocket. He displayed the contents to her in the palm of his hand. She lifted the bag up and gasped.

"Sour gummy bears. How did you remember? Thanks."

"Well, you might not want to thank me until after you taste them. I'm sure I squished them in my attempt to get here. I apologize for that."

She laughed. "Gummy bears are already squished, silly." He joined her in her revelry seconds before they walked up to the cashier.

"My treat," he said, before she uttered a word.

"Are you sure?"

"Order what you want besides you're a starving college student. I'm a paid employee now."

She chortled at his grin and mouthed her thanks to him before placing her order. The young girl behind the register stared starry-eyed at him as he stepped up to the counter. He placed his order and then whipped out his credit card, proceeding to pay when the cashier's hand touched his. She gave him a shy smile with a quick giggle before she zipped his card through the scanner and placed the card with the receipt on the countertop with a pen, for him to sign. Clay glanced across his shoulder at Marisole to find her aware of the cashier's flirtations with him. He grimaced as he signed the piece of paper and, instead of picking it up and handing it to the cashier as he always did; he slid it across the counter toward her, to avoid contact. He met her frown seconds before he picked up his own receipt, folded it and placed it into his wallet.

"I see your fan base hasn't changed," Marisole said, a side smirk, replacing her usual smile.

He snapped his wallet closed, sliding the object down his back pocket. "I can't help who finds me attractive."

"Apparently that's the general population," she teased.

"Present company excluded."

"Yes." His heart thudded to a stop. "You know how I feel about..." She left the thought hanging but he knew what she wanted to say.

She was going to end her sentence with the word womanizers. She still considered him one though he had not dated in the past four months. Granted, his description of dating was different than hers. She considered a date, dinner and a movie. He, on the other hand, only wanted sex with alcohol optional.

By her description, he supposed he was a womanizer. He decided four months ago that he was done with casual flings. He would solely date those he was serious about and the only woman who fit that description was Marisole. The irony was that she wanted nothing to do with him besides basic friendship and even that seemed tentative, at the moment.

"I'm not that anymore," he said as they picked up their plates and walked outside, claiming a table off to one side of the building. The temperature, in the low seventies, made it a beautiful day to enjoy nature and a good sandwich, too.

"Reformed, are we?" She placed her tray onto the table and quickly apologized. "I didn't mean to make you feel bad. As I said before, your life is your life and none of my business."

Yet, he wanted their lives intertwined. How could he explain it to her without her taking it the wrong way? "You didn't make me feel bad. I realize you're right. I have been doing a lot of casual dating. Now that I have graduated and am working in a good job, I no longer want that lifestyle. But let's take the focus off me and talk about you. Have you found anyone, yet?"

She unfolded the wrapping from her sub and snorted. "Who, me? Nooo. I'm too focused on my last year in college. I don't have time to date. Besides, I always find losers. I think I'm a magnet for them."

"Maybe you're searching for the wrong type of men or... maybe you've already found the right one but you don't recognize him."

"Who? Joey?" She giggled. "He always said that if he didn't have Paige and we were out of college, he'd pursue me."

"Don't blame him," Clay muttered under his breath between bites. The idea of Joey and Marisole together stung him in the gut. He knew Joey liked Marisole but he never knew how serious he was. Marisole, apparently, had a point, when it came to Joey. If she dated Clay, Joey might become jealous. That wouldn't work for either of them.

Clay bit a little too hard into his sandwich with his next bite. His tooth grazed the tip of his tongue, thinking it was lettuce and he hissed under his breath.

She tore a chunk out of her sub. Clay's eyes darted, riveted to her mouth when her tongue snaked out and swiped a stray glob of mayo at one corner. "What about you? You dating anyone you're serious about?" Forgetting his own sandwich, he stared at her while she continued eating. She took a sip from her soda can, dropped it onto the table and stopped all movement when he didn't respond.

"Clay? You okay?" She repeated his name twice. When that didn't work, she reached across the table and placed her hand over his. Her soft skin touching his zinged pleasant tingles of awareness straight to his groin. His head jerked back as reality sank in. She had asked him a question but he had no clue what it was.

"Hi." She laughed. "Welcome back."

If she only knew where his mind went. Never mind. It was better she didn't know such things until they had a more solid, intimate relationship.

He shook his head. "Sorry. Had my mind on other things."

"I can see that. Must've been a good place."

"Yeah, actually it was."

"With your girlfriend? The one you're seriously dating that you haven't mentioned yet?"

"No. I'm not dating anyone at the moment."

"Oh? Too bad. I was going to kid you about some tight skirt you met at work that you can't keep your hands off," she teased.

He winked. "No. No one like that, at least not yet."

"Well, good. That means there's still time."

He almost choked on the bite he took. Instead, he forced it down, chasing it with a long swig of soda. "Time for what?" he croaked, hoping she meant that his single status gave her a chance to pursue him. If she wanted him, he would offer himself on a platter, with the ability to sample him in any way she preferred.

"For you to find a real woman. One who will treat you right. One you can spend your entire life with. Isn't that what you want, Clay?"

He mumbled under his breath, "More than ever."

She finished her meal and passed the napkin over her mouth. "So, why haven't you found the right one?"

Because he found her and she was sitting right in front of him. He shoved the last bite of his sandwich into his mouth. "Because I've been wasting my time on meaningless experiences instead of concentrating on what I ultimately want."

"You'll find her, Clay. She's out there waiting for you to discover her. I know she is."

Marisole was right. The woman he wanted was available. The question was, what did he need to do to gain her attention?

The rest of the conversation veered toward her remaining classes, her upcoming exams and her job. Clay inquired about her plans after graduation.

"I think I want to be in your shoes when I graduate."

"Come again?"

"I mean, you had a job and an apartment lined up when you graduated. How much more perfect can that be?"

"I wanted to have a plan."

"And you got one. Bravo! That's how I want it to be when I step off that stage. I want a plan of my own, you know."

"You will. You're smart, pretty and talented. Any company would be happy to have you on board."

"Did you just call me pretty?"

He nodded. "You know you are, Marisole." Yet, he was wrong. Marisole was more than pretty. She was cute, charming and fun to be with. She was also sexy, as hell. Mentioning any of these alternate descriptions, though, would have had her running for the hills so he kept quiet when, instead, he wanted to sing her praises and tell her how he truly felt about her. In fact, why didn't he? What was the worst that could happen? Her saying, "no" would devastate him but, eventually, he'd get over it. Maybe. It might very well take a lifetime to get past her rejection of him but if he didn't say anything, he'd never find out. This was it. This was the moment that would change their history. He took a deep breath.

"Marisole, there's something I want to say."

Just then, her phone rang. She opened her bag and pulled out her cellphone. With a look of remorse, she said, "It's Joey. I have to take it. I'm sorry. We're working on a project, together."

Reality slapped him in the face like a stinky, wet towel. Damn. There was no way Joey would accept them having a relationship, beyond friendship. If Joey knew Clay was pursuing Marisole, he'd deck him if not do something else more drastic. Clay knew how Joey felt about him, when it came to stable relationships. Joey's warnings to stay away from Marisole echoed in his mind and dashed all hopes of pursuing his dream girl.

Marisole ended the call and slipped her phone back into her purse. "Joey says Hi, by the way."

Through the sudden knot forming in his stomach, Clay forced a smile.

"You wanted to say something to me, before? I'm sorry I interrupted you. Go on."

"It was nothing. Actually, I forgot what it was about. Maybe it'll come to me, later."

"Okay. This was really nice, Clay. Thank you."

"You're welcome."

Clay gave himself one last thrill and hugged Marisole goodbye before he made his way back to the car. He grunted as he got closer to the car, ruminating over what he could never have but still trying to find a way to win her. There was no getting anything past Joey and the last thing Clay wanted to do was keep a relationship with his dream girl a secret. In fact, the opposite was true. If he was lucky enough to find himself in a relationship with Marisole, he'd want to shout it over the rooftops. Having her, as his partner in life, was akin to winning the Powerball, elusive but possible if you were that one in two-hundred and ninety-two million.

Despite these odds and his wounded heart, he contacted Marisole over the next few months and ran into her at Joey's yearly holiday party. He also sent her a Christmas card with a poinsettia pin, this time, instead of an actual plant. She had two thriving plants in her dorm room and begged off any more, stating there was no more room for them. He was glad his Poinsettia plants were alive, expecting that every time she looked at them, they would remind her of him.

As the months passed and Marisole's final school term arrived, Clay was introduced to a new female co-worker. Dana was unlike any woman he met. She was tall and slim with legs that went up to her neck. The woman was gloriously beautiful and even her bronze skin beamed sexiness. She did things with the stem of a cherry he'd never seen before. Despite the strict workplace fraternization rules, they engaged in vigorous sex in the back of his truck one day, waiting for the office to open.

Dana adjusted her skirt, after their sensual rendezvous, and opened the truck door, "See you later, lover." She winked and wiggled her curvaceous ass as she crossed the parking lot to the main building. Damn. She was hot and Clay needed the lay. He couldn't wait any longer for Marisole. Not after realizing that Joey would never give them a chance. After Clay made his decision about Marisole, he waited and waited for the right woman, convincing himself he was wrong about Marisole, in the meantime, and then Dana walked into his life on red, three-inch stilettos. Damn that woman for having fine, succulent, legs. He'd happily feast on them every night if she'd let him.

Despite his feelings for Dana, Clay was loathe to delete Marisole's picture from his phone. When Dana found it one day, among his pictures, he lied and told her it was only a friend from his past, one he contacted every so often. Dana made sure Clay knew exactly how she felt about Marisole. She also informed Clay that Marisole was beautiful and that she better never find him staring at her the way he stared at Dana.

It was best to keep the two females apart, not that he'd seen much of Marisole since Joey's holiday party. The phone calls and text messages stopped shortly after he met Dana. There was no way he was screwing up this relationship. Now that he met Dana, he wanted to keep her, certain she had to be the one for him since Marisole wasn't.

Dana was adventurous and a thrill-seeker. Clay had never been more scared in his life.

Dating Dana was different than any of his previous experiences and, for that, Clay was happy. Dana had Clay doing things he never thought he'd agree to. After bungee-jumping, hang gliding, and jumping off a cliff into the ocean, Clay thought he was done until Dana got him into a clear glass elevator, dropped his pants and gave him the most thrilling BJ of his life- one that had him grabbing the walls and hollering for mercy. Holy hell! To say the woman was adventurous was putting it mildly. Yet, as much as Clay enjoyed Dana taking charge of their dates, he wanted to take the wheel more times than he cared to admit.

As much as he liked Dana, there were times he couldn't stop thinking of Marisole. He was ashamed to admit it, but it was often Marisole's body he caressed, her moans he heard and her sultry lips he sought in the middle of the night when Dana was on top of him. When he saw Marisole on campus, during his visits with Joey, he couldn't stop staring at her, wondering if he made a mistake.

Though Dana was a constant adventure, Marisole was magical. As much as he tried to convince himself that Marisole was not the one for him, he couldn't get the gorgeous beauty out of his mind. At first, he thought the attraction was solely based on Marisole's unattainable status and that it was only the thrill of the chase he wanted, but he was wrong. He knew that if he was fortunate enough to capture Marisole's heart, he would never let her go. She would be his, forever, no matter what he had to do to keep her.

It was Marisole's sweet smile that brought him to his knees.

13 ~Marisole~

It was finals week and the end of the spring term and Marisole had no idea how they made it. She and Paige had already made plans to move in together after graduation, if nothing else panned out for Marisole before then. Marisole applied to several jobs, but she wasn't as fortunate as Clay when it came to landing one. She'd been selected for a few interviews and was followed up on by several others but there had been no interest yet which was fine with her as she still had her job at the retail store. As much as she'd love to hand in her two weeks' notice, at least she still had a steady stream of income to pay her scant bills, which would surely increase after graduation.

She held the paper graduation invites in her hands. Her school still believed in handing out paper invitations for their graduation ceremonies. Although online invitations were possible, the majority of the school's invitations were mailed out. She reviewed her list of invitees, checking them twice like the popular jolly, old, saint bearing a red hat and reindeer who came to visit good children on Christmas Eve but she did a double-take when she came across Clay's name.

Should she invite him? He had a girlfriend now. According to Joey, he was very busy with the beautiful amazon.

The problem was, if she sent Clay an invite, he would likely invite her, too. He did, after all, invite Marisole to his graduation ceremony and she figured she needed to return the favor but the prospect of witnessing Clay with a woman draped on his arm was definitely not on Marisole's bucket list. He could parade women around all day, any day but on her special day-no- she didn't want that. Maybe she'd let Joey invite him, instead, and save Clay's invitation for another guest. Yep, that's what Marisole would do. Instead of two invites, Clay would receive one. Besides, one was all he needed to attend the ceremony.

A fleeting fantasy image of a gorgeous male, unknown to anyone in her small group of friends, and standing by her side, passed through her mind and caused a grin to slide up the corners of her mouth. If only she could rustle up someone like that for her graduation day. She needed a tall, hot looking male to rival Clay. Yet, she had no idea where she'd find such a man. She wasn't one to frequent bars, trolling for graduation dates and she couldn't picture where else one could pick up a guy last minute without scrolling through escort sites or worse, dating apps that often ended up in one night stands. But the look on

Clay's face when he took one glance at Mr. Hottie standing by her side after graduation would be priceless.

Why she cared what Clay thought of her, she didn't know. The last time they spoke was by text message sometime in January, before he met Dana.

Paige waltzed through the door and pointed at the table Marisole sat at. "You done with that list, yet?"

"No but I will be. Just a few more guests to consider and then I'm done."

"Well, the most important people will be there. You know, Joey and me."

Marisole playfully swatted Paige with an invite she held in her hand, as she passed by.

Paige squealed out loud. "Hey! I'm just saying.'"

"And you know Joey is inviting Clay which brings me to another subject. Clay is more than likely going to bring Dana. Are you okay with that?"

Marisole shrugged her shoulders. "Why wouldn't I be?"

"Come on, girl. You like Clay, don't you?" When Marisole didn't respond, Paige continued. "You've never met Dana. She's nice but Joey swears she's not the one for Clay." Paige's eyebrows shot up. "Oh no, don't worry, Joey doesn't know about your feelings for Clay. I never said anything."

"Paige, Clay and I are...we're...well, I'm not sure what we are but he has no interest in me. Besides, he has Dana, which I'm sure is a lovely girl."

Paige snorted then rolled her eyes. "Yeah, wait till you meet her."

"She can't be that bad."

Paige looked directly at her before she sauntered out of the room. "She's not the one meant for Clay."

Marisole couldn't help wondering who was meant for Clay if Dana wasn't. She refocused her efforts on printing out the names of the last few guests to invite after Paige shut her bedroom door.

After several more minutes of getting nowhere with finishing up the guest list, Marisole decided to leave the dorm to give Paige some privacy. She had been cooped up on the sofa for hours and the urge to get out of the place to stretch her legs and get a bit of fresh air nagged at her. Besides, it had been almost a week since either of them had checked the mailbox.

She gathered her belongings and folded them neatly into a stack at the end of the coffee table, placing a photo magnet that doubled as a paperweight on top of it. The magnet contained a picture of her and Paige, one that she treasured as they both looked great in the picture. Not particularly photogenic, Marisole only kept pictures of herself where she looked halfway decent and destroyed the others, making sure they were cleared out of the recycle bin, too, lest someone have blackmail material ready and able to use. She snickered at the idea, knowing that wasn't the real reason she deleted the pictures but it made for a comical excuse should anyone ask.

Images of Clay intruded while she plodded out the door. She stared at her cellphone, her fingers hovering over the buttons, considering whether or not she should call him. Yet, why in the world would she call him? He had a girlfriend now. If he wanted to talk to anyone, it would be her not Marisole, that he should go to first. Her only excuse for calling him was to hear his soothing, manly tone of voice. She loved listening to his voice and missed it. Besides, he was a good listener and always had such great advice to give. As much as she wanted to talk to him, she couldn't come up with a real reason to. She dropped her phone back into her pocket and kept moving, aiming for the on-campus mailboxes, and almost reaching her destination when her phone sounded. Sliding it out with an enthusiastic revving up of her heartbeat, she stared at the number calling her and realized it was not Clay. Her heartbeat took a nosedive as she pressed the green button and said hello.

Ending the call several minutes later, she stood, stunned and unable to move. She blinked her eyes several times and wondered if her feet remained on the ground. The call was unexpected but it held great news. She had just accepted the job the caller proposed. The only problem was that the job was in another state and she'd have to move. Their offer, though, was too good to be true. It came with a stipend and an apartment. She couldn't pass it up. In fact, she remained shocked she was given the opportunity, to begin with, but the caller was insistent, explaining that because of her stellar work with Helping Hands, the corporate office wanted to keep her on but this time in another capacity and with a regular paycheck.

After collecting the few ads she found in their mailbox along with two letters for Paige, she dashed home to throw open the door and tell Paige her good news until it dawned on her the impact it would have on her. If she left, Paige would have no roommate to share the household expenses. It wasn't fair to leave Paige like that but she had to take advantage of the opportunity given to her. Yet, hurting Paige and leaving her to fend for herself was the last thing she wanted to do. She shut the door behind her, dropped the sparse pieces of mail onto the coffee table and trudged down the hallway, calling out her friend's name.

Paige's reaction to Marisole's news; however, was not what Marisole expected. She was elated for her friend's good fortune and advised her to take it, saying she would be fine on her own. Her parents would help her, anyway so it was not too big of a loss, though, she said, she would miss Marisole dearly. When Marisole asked her not to tell anyone she was leaving, Paige's eyebrows drew up and she asked why. Marisole couldn't come up with a good excuse, just that, for some reason, she didn't want Clay to know she was leaving. Yet, she didn't speak this last part out loud. She assured Paige she would tell Joey later but she didn't want anyone else but her to know, at the moment, and she wanted to be the one to tell others her good news. Paige nodded in agreement, telling her that she would leave all the glory of spreading the news about her new job to Marisole.

If someone asked Marisole why she didn't want Clay to know she was leaving, she wouldn't know what to tell them. Clay was involved in a relationship and she didn't want to put a wedge or a damper on things, not that spreading this news would mean anything significant to Clay, anyway, or would it? All she knew was that she liked Clay a lot and she couldn't watch the elation in his face turn to anything else when she told him she was moving. Besides, she was never any good at goodbyes and with Clay, their parting would be final. It wasn't the same with Paige and Joey, who she expected to invite over to her new place shortly after moving in. Those two were permanent friends in her small circle but, for some reason, Clay always remained an outsider. She was hopeful that things would change between them over the years but they never did. Keeping him lingering on was not only damaging to her heart but useless for their situation, whatever that might be.

When graduation day finally arrived, Marisole was prepared to find Clay with Dana at the ceremony but she wasn't prepared for how pretty Dana was. Dana was tall with impossibly flawless skin, a perky nose, and chiseled facial features. She could've been picked straight off a magazine cover with her uncommon beauty and when Dana opened her mouth to speak, musical notes intertwined with her lyrical voice. Marisole couldn't help staring at the couple, sizing them up to determine their compatibility. Dana playfully touched Clay throughout the beginning, before the graduates got on stage. While they waited in their seats, Dana stroked his cheek with several fingers, leaned over and whispered in his ear, while running her hand through his thick hair. She leaned back and giggled to something Clay said. They were the perfect, cute couple and this made Marisole sick to her stomach.

Marisole swiveled on her heel and drew in several deep breaths while Joey patted her hand and asked if she was okay. She nodded, attempting a small smile at the same time, to shoo away his concern. This was a time for Joey to celebrate his grand accomplishment not to worry about her. Besides Clay was some school-girl crush she should've overcome years ago. The idea of her and Clay, together, was ludicrous, she told herself. The problem was her heart and her body didn't want to believe what her brain desperately tried to convince them.

Clay smiled over at her and Joey and waved at him while Dana looked on. Marisole took a good long look at Dana's outfit while a sting of jealousy thumped through areas of her heart, zinging the nasty sensation back and forth across crevices like a pinball machine in use. Dana's dress fit her like a glove, hugging every curve she had on her for Clay's entertainment and enjoyment. She also wore gorgeous but ridiculously high stiletto heels that Marisole could only dream of balancing her wide width feet on. Marisole swallowed down the dry lump forming in the back of her throat while attempting to calm her revved up anxiety. It wasn't enough that she was already stressed with the happy fact of her graduation, the new job and the apartment that lay in her future but now she had to witness the beautiful gal Clay picked for himself. Granted, Marisole knew all along that she wasn't Clay's type but to witness the confirmation right in front of her almost knocked the wind out of her. She had hoped she was wrong regarding her suspicions regarding Clay's preferences but with Dana sitting next to him there was no way to refute the truth.

When they called out Joey's name, Marisole stood and clapped, shouting his name with a happy smile plastered across her face. She glanced over at Clay who was also standing. With two fingers in his mouth, he whistled a high tone into the air before clapping his hands together, enthusiastically, for his best friend. Dana also stood next to Clay, grabbing ahold of his hand when he sat back down.

Several students later, it was Marisole's turn. She walked up the three steps to the stage and smiled widely as she spotted the president in the middle of the floor. Almost four years ago she set foot on campus with a wide-eyed Joey leading her around, showing her all the sights, sharing tips with her on the best professors and the ones to avoid. She was younger back then and more naive but it was a great time in her life. Choosing this particular school was one of the best decisions she made and the other was volunteering for Helping Hands. For the most part, she enjoyed her time on campus, she made a great friend in Paige and she loved working with the women at the crisis center. She had gained many friends and shared many wonderful experiences and if she could do it all over again, she would. But today, she was glad she didn't have to, for she was presently walking across the stage, shaking the president's hand and receiving his congratulations. She only wished her mom was here. She knew wherever her mom was now in the vast universe, she would be proud of her. Marisole had always believed there was something more than the one life a person received. She had to. She loved her mom too much to think she was gone permanently.

Marisole had no other family members, not knowing if her wretched dad was alive or dead. Besides, she wouldn't have wanted him here to celebrate with her something he had never been a part of. Last night, she revealed her amazing career opportunity to Joey. He swore to keep it a secret from Clay until she decided to reveal it to him. If she ever did. For now, the only ones who knew about her exciting job opportunity were Paige and Joey and Marisole was happy to keep it that way.

Clay approached her after the ceremony. Instead of a hug, he offered her a handshake with his congratulations seconds before he introduced his girlfriend, Dana. If it were possible, the woman was more beautiful up close. Dana shook her hand and belted out words to her in a musical tone of voice that had mini-boulders plummeting Marisole's fragile heart into pieces. Marisole simply stared at her, not knowing what Dana said but utterly fascinated with the female, unable to tear her eyes away from her image while confused about where in the world Dana came from. If nothing else, it was good to know that Clay was happy and that he would continue being so long after Marisole was gone...

Joey and Marisole soon met up with Paige, whose graduation ceremony was later that same day. They cheered for her up on the stage and Joey gave her a bouquet of red roses shortly after the ceremony was completed. Then they all climbed into Marisole's car to celebrate at a local restaurant with a few of their close friends. Arriving at their happy hour, several in their party ordered drinks and appetizers. The frenzied, energetic conversation made everyone smile, including Marisole who couldn't stop glancing over at Dana. Though no one knew her, Dana, somehow, fell easily into conversation, her cheery laughter and her great sense of humor falling into place with the others in their group. Marisole, though, remained stunned at how perfect Dana seemed.

"Here, Mare. I hope you like it." Clay's words interrupted her thoughts. She turned toward him and received the small box with a ribbon tied to the top of it.

"What? What is this?"

"A gift for your graduation."

"Oh? You didn't have to get me anything. Thank you."

He grinned. "No problem. Open it."

She lifted the top off the box and laughed as she picked up the grocery store gift card.

"I figured you and Paige might need a little help for your first month in your new apartment. It's really expensive living on your own and your gift card helped me so I thought I'd return the favor."

Marisole turned the gift card in her hands before she replied. "Thanks, Clay." She dropped it into the box and closed the lid. "It will come in handy."

"Glad I could help. Oh and here's a card from Dana and me."

He slipped a large envelope into her hand before he took off. Marisole pulled the card out of the envelope and read it. It held a funny sentiment with their heartfelt congratulations inside. It was nice of Clay but the fact that Clay and Dana were not only handing out cards together but signing them, as well, made the fact that they were in a serious relationship more real. Marisole didn't know why this surprised her. She supposed she wasn't prepared for the fact that Clay had moved on.

Despite the blow Clay, unwittingly, dealt her, Marisole enjoyed the rest of the night, knowing she was taking off on a plane in three days. This weekend was the last that she would spend with Paige and Joey until they could all meet up again so she aimed to enjoy herself as much as possible before she braved her future, on her own.

She smiled when Clay challenged her to a game of darts. Having no idea how to play the game, she made her best effort, cheering with the first and only bullseye she made and, in the end, buying him a beer when he won.

"Good game," she said, shaking his hand. She turned to walk away yet he hadn't let go of her hand. When she whipped her head to look at him she caught a strange look on his face that was hard to describe. It seemed a cross between regret and reluctance, two things she'd never witnessed with Clay before.

"Can I have my hand back?" she asked with a smile.

"Yeah, sure." He squeezed her hand once before he opened his fingers enough for her to retrieve her hand. Instead of turning to leave, they stared at each other for several more long seconds while a voice nagged at her that Dana might notice. What were they doing? Their long looks could be interpreted as something different, a subject neither of them approached or opened up for discussion. It was not proper to continue studying someone else's man. Yes, that was what Clay essentially was- someone else's. There was no use pining over someone who was already taken and Marisole was definitely not one to step back into the shadows and wait for anyone to make up their mind about her. Clay had Dana and Dana deserved respect. Marisole broke eye contact and turned away. She felt the heat of his lingering stare as she walked back to her seat.

She heard Clay's voice boom behind her. "Anyone else want to challenge me?"

Paige piped up. "I will." She sashayed up to Clay, receiving a swat on her bottom from Joey for her efforts. He winked at her when she turned to retort.

The game played out well with Paige doing a better job than Marisole's sad attempt. With the very last dart thrown, Paige spoke up. "This one is for Marisole, to redeem her loss." Paige threw her hands up in the air as she won the game. "Yeah, take that Clay. Girl's rule!" Marisole ran up to her. They ended their celebration with congratulatory hugs, high-pitched squeals, and a high-five.

"My turn." A sultry voice behind Marisole interrupted their calamity. Marisole scooted out of the way to find Dana gliding up to Clay.

She pulled him down into a big, wet kiss and an even bigger production amidst the whooping and hollering of the men at their table. She continued with a hug and simulated groping of his body, running her hands down the back of his jeans and squeezing his firm buns to shouts of "Get a room, you two," and "Oh yeah man, go for it." The catcalls and whistles soon dissipated as each picked up a dart and started the game.

Marisole bent her head toward Paige and whispered. "Clay found a good one."

Paige grabbed her drink and swished the liquid inside it while she spoke. "Smoke and mirrors, hun." She dropped her head back and let the liquid gold slide down her throat.

"What do you mean?"

"It ain't all that it's cracked up to be. She's trying too hard. He's already having problems with her."

"Really? But they act like such a cute couple."

Paige looked straight at her. "What did I just tell you? Looks can be deceiving. He told Joey he's hung up on someone else but Dana is fun. He's not serious about her. He's told her that, too, but she doesn't seem to care. She wants him."

"Even though he can't have a serious relationship with her?"

Paige tossed her glass back onto the counter. "Uh-huh."

Marisole blinked her eyes several times. "Wow. I thought they were an item. The way she hangs on to him..."

"Yes, but who is hanging on to whom? If Clay was in love with her, don't you think he'd be the one hanging on to her, instead?"

"I see what you mean. But who is he hung up on? Did he say?"

"No, but it seems like someone who doesn't like him or something like that."

Marisole frowned. Clay liked someone who didn't like him? Incredible. More importantly, how was that possible? Everyone liked Clay. He was a ladies man, complete with the ability to charm the pants off a woman. Besides that, he was sincere, honest and he cared about people. The fact that there was a woman out there that didn't like Clay didn't make sense but the irony of it made Marisole smile. Maybe Clay had met his match, after all.

14 ~Clay~

Dana's hands were all over him, *again.* He told her several times over the past few months that he wasn't interested in anything long-term with her though he couldn't help adding that he found her fun to be with. It was the truth. He liked spending time with Dana. She was not only entertaining but also a great distraction. She also loved sex, a fact that Clay could easily live with except for those few times he felt guilty afterward, contemplating the one female he really wanted to be with.

Yet, the one woman he envisioned a future with sat next to Paige at the end of the table, completely unaware of his interest. Since taking a seat, he caught her glancing his way a few times while he was playing darts but where her eyes aimed, it seemed more likely she was looking at Dana instead of him.

The title girlfriend was one Dana came up with since they spent much time together. The word girlfriend seemed too romantic and too permanent, neither of which Clay wanted from Dana. He racked his brain for another term yet he couldn't come up with anything plausible. At a loss for an alternate description of their relationship except for friends with benefits, which made Dana extremely upset one night, he settled for girlfriend and boyfriend since it appeased her. Truly, he didn't care what title she came up with except when it came to Marisole's perception of their relationship. More than anything, he wanted to disclose to Marisole the truth about the relationship with Dana but they hadn't talked in a while and he imagined the news of him in a relationship didn't hit Marisole well since Clay was never serious about anyone.

Unable to take the suspense any longer, he swung by Paige and Marisole, congratulating Paige again for her swift dart work and asking to speak with Marisole.

Marisole lifted her eyebrows and pointed to herself with a questioning look on her face.

"Yes, you. I want to talk to you." He walked toward the back of the restaurant and glanced over his shoulder to check to see if she was following. She slid off her barstool and shrugged her shoulders at Paige before she took off.

He sighed, unsure how to start the ultimate conversation they needed to change a few things for them. At the end of their chat, she'd either run in the opposite direction or accept him. Which path she chose was up to her though he hoped it would be the latter.

Marisole crossed her arms in front of her and asked, "What did you want to talk to me about?"

"Look, I know that you know I am in a relationship with Dana."

"Yeah, I'm a bit surprised because you don't do relationships."

He looked her squarely in the eyes. "Not unless I'm with the right woman."

"Well, I guess she's the right one for you, Clay. Congratulations. I thought I'd never see it. I'm glad you're happy." He grasped her arm as she turned to walk away.

"You don't understand. I'm not in a relationship with Dana. Well, yes I am, but it's not what you think."

She snorted and then gave him an amused smile. "Isn't that what people say when they get caught?"

His eyebrows scrunched together. "What? Listen, I'm trying to be serious with you."

"And I'm saying Congratulations. I think it's great, now can you let me go, please?" She tried shaking her hand out of his grasp but that only made him hold on tighter.

"My God woman, I'm trying to talk to you! Do you know you can be stubborn?"

She stepped back, her mouth opening at an odd angle, "Are you yelling at me, Clay Evans?"

He shook his head and released her hand. "If you want to leave, then just go. I only wanted you to know that Dana and I aren't serious."

Marisole tilted her head to one side. "Does she know that? Because you two look really good together." She lowered her voice. "I mean it, Clay. She really likes you and I think it's great. You should have someone good in your life. You deserve it."

He lowered his shoulders and sighed. "Just go, Mare. I'm sorry to have bothered you."

She touched his upper arm. The spot where her fingers lay warmed through his skin, prickling sudden awareness in the sensitive nerves surrounding the area. She spoke softly, "What's wrong? You know that you can talk to me."

"I don't want to be with her."

"Then why are you?"

Because I can't have you. Clay stared at her, the words he wanted to say at the tip of his tongue. He closed his mouth before he had the chance to regret spilling the secrets held within his heart. He loved Marisole. He wanted her. He had given more hints to her than he had to anyone and she hadn't noticed a single one. Marisole loved her independence and freedom. She had a bright future ahead of her, no matter what she chose to do. She didn't need a boyfriend hanging around her, messing up her life.

He lowered his head and lied, unable to face her with the words he forced out of his mouth. "I don't know why."

"Maybe you should tell her the truth. No one likes being strung along."

He tried to tell Dana the truth but she didn't accept it. She'd been through some rough relationships in the past, knew Clay was a good guy and latched on to him, and now she was unwilling to let him go. Rejected by the one woman he adored; Clay settled for Dana's good company including the warmth her supple body gave him during his lonely nights. She kept his bed warm and his thoughts off of Marisole. He enjoyed spending time with Dana and she was good, for now.

Marisole winked. "You're a ladies man, Clay. You'll find the woman you're meant to be with."

He peered into her eyes. "I only want to be one lady's man."

She patted his shoulder. "You'll find her. Trust me, you will." Marisole swiveled on her heel.

Clay's thoughts lingered in his mind as he watched Marisole reclaim the seat next to Paige.

But I already have.

***

After an intense, long weekend, it was finally Monday. Clay sat at his computer desk with his head in his hands, lamenting all that occurred in the last couple of days and trying to figure out what to do next. He still held feelings for Marisole and he wasn't about to let go of the possibility of them, their lives intertwined at some point in the near future. How could he convince Marisole to give him a chance and how did he start that conversation with her?

He looked up at the computer screen, knowing he was supposed to be checking inventory instead of contemplating what-if's. Yet his heart wasn't in his job duties today, not after the rough weekend he had. He kept replaying the conversation he had with Marisole on Friday afternoon. Marisole didn't get it. She was the one he wanted to be with. Yet, nothing he said or did convinced her. She wasn't going to hurt Joey. In the meantime, Clay was the one in pain.

Clay rolled his head back and forth in his hands, groaning under his breath. Marisole. Beautiful, hard-headed Marisole with a glorious ass he'd love to grab, a sexy as sin body he'd love to fondle and lush, full lips he'd love to smother with his own. My God, the woman was gorgeous and she didn't know it. Tawdry images of her found him up at night sporting a hardon he had to cure every time. She had no idea the effect she had on him and the hours he spent picturing the life he wanted with her. If only he could take their friendship to the next level and date her. She would be his first real date that led to something beyond casual dates. With Dana, he was hopeful their dates led to something else but after some time he realized she wasn't what he wanted and that he was fooling himself biding his time with other women when there was only one female who held his interest. No one else would do. He had to try with Marisole.

Clay often envisioned his future, preparing for what he wanted in life and making a list of goals for what he wanted to work toward. He found himself listing Marisole every time, his dreams including them, together, working toward the same common goals and outcomes they were passionate about. Whether she liked it or not, his future included her. It was about time she knew it.

With new resolve thrumming through his heart, Clay leaped out of his chair. Leaning over his desk, he closed down the programs currently open on his computer and then shut down the computer, itself. There was no way he was staying at work when there were words to be said to a certain stubborn, bull-headed, gorgeous woman.

Clay was going to find her at Paige's and talk to her until she came to her senses and realized how much she meant to him. Before the day was through he resolved their relationship would either shatter into a billion pieces with no hope for recovery or they would take the next step and start dating. He crossed his fingers and prayed for the latter. He needed Marisole in his life.

15 ~Marisole~

Seven a.m. Monday morning and Marisole was not ready. She slammed her hand down on the alarm clock, a little too heavy on the touch, and then threw her arms up in the air and yawned noisily, groaning out her discord at having been woken up from her comfortable bed. A light knocking sounded at her door and Paige slipped through it, sliding her body underneath the bedsheets beside her.

"Why do you have to goo?" she whined by her ear, her arms wrapping Marisole into a warm embrace.

"I know." Marisole groaned. "I don't want to go either but I have to. I'm going to miss you."

"Me too. I'm going to miss you so much. You can come back anytime to visit your car."

Marisole grinned. She gave her car to Paige since Paige didn't have one. Although Paige's parents offered to buy her a brand new car as her graduation gift; Paige opted to rescue Marisole's prized possession instead, telling Marisole it would make her feel closer to her even though they were miles apart. The sentiment brought fresh tears to Marisole's eyes. Instead of paying to transport the car to another state, Marisole figured she would save the money to buy a good used one near her new residence. Paige reassured Marisole the car would get a lot of love and it would be shared between her and Joey.

Marisole slipped into the bathroom for the last time, taking stuff down and folding it, packing it all neatly into her suitcase. She changed into the clothes she had hanging up in the closet and stuffed her suitcase with all the little extras she couldn't pack away until the final day appeared. She walked out into the kitchen and sat at a barstool while Paige finished cooking her famous blueberry pancakes. Grabbing the bottle of syrup, Marisole squirted a generous amount on her plate, slopping the syrup over her sausages before capping the bottle and dropping it onto the countertop. Picking up a fork and knife, she took her first slice, brought it up to her lips and moaned as she chewed.

"Mmm, this is so good. Thank you, Paige."

"No problem, roomie. You know your leaving was a good thing in a sense because now Joey can move in."

If Marisole had a pillow she'd toss it at Paige, instead, she just glared at her with a smirk set to her mouth.

"I'm just kidding. I really am going to miss you and I'm a little scared with Joey being here. I mean, what if he's messy?"

"You'll deal with it. You love him too much."

She smiled and nodded her head. "You're right. There's nothing the man can do wrong."

Marisole shoved a forkful of pancake into her mouth. "Oh yeah there is. You just ignore it."

Paige rolled a napkin up and tossed it at her. Marisole dodged it before it hit her arm, letting the ball of paper fall to the floor. Paige laughed as she took the seat next to her. They chatted for an hour before Marisole got up, washed the dishes and returned to packing the rest of her items.

Getting out of her car for the very last time, Joey and Paige accompanied Marisole to the airline terminal and said their goodbyes. Tears were shed and laughter abounded as they parted ways, all promising to keep in touch. Marisole was never any good at goodbyes and she hated these moments because they brought on so much sorrow. She watched her friends as they walked away, hand in hand, Paige holding onto her old keychain which bore her new car keys.

"Bye old friends," Marisole murmured under her breath. She caught Paige's wave last minute before she turned the corner, out of her sight. Marisole let the tears flow, swiping at them as they ran down in streams across her cheeks. She was happy her friends had set aside the time to take her to the airport and see her off.

She considered texting Clay, the idea of saying goodbye to him in a message form more appealing to her than having to speak to him in person, but then she thought better of it. Sometime during the weekend, he had broken it off with Dana, an ending to a relationship that didn't go over really well with Dana, Joey said. Clay needed his privacy and alone time now, more than ever, she figured. Besides, she was never any good at goodbyes. Once she got settled in, she might consider contacting him but, for now, she'd let him be.

***

Clay raced through the streets, pumping his foot down on the accelerator till he figured the car was now flying. If his car wasn't airborne yet, he didn't know what would give it wings. He concentrated on getting to his destination despite all the warning bells sounding in his head at his recklessness. If the cops didn't ticket him and he didn't end up in an accident, he might have a chance to make it to the airport on time to catch Marisole.

Why did she leave without saying good-bye? When Paige told him she was gone, he almost stopped breathing. She left Clay without him having a chance to tell her how much she meant to him. It wasn't fair and it wasn't going to happen, not if he had a say.

He finally swerved right on the last stretch of asphalt to the airport. If he had to drive his car straight onto the runway to stop her, he'd do it. She had to know how special she was to him.

Blaring his horn, he swiped the car left then right zig-zagging around a tourist or elderly person. Whoever it was behind him keeping up with the speed of a bicyclist could eat his dust. There was no way he'd miss Marisole's escape.

Screeching to a halt in front of the main entrance, he threw open the car door and then slammed it hard, skipping up onto the pavement and breaking into a run as he flew through the sliding glass doors of the building, leaving the car, the stunned valets and the lagging pedestrians behind. Never a sprinter, he ran as fast as he could, unconcerned with whether he had the capability to race through the throngs of people who showed up just to stand in his way. Delivering acrobatic moves he never thought possible of his solid, inflexible body, he maneuvered around every obstacle thrown at him, almost running into a pole as he bent left to avoid impact like a scene in the Matrix.

With no chance to check his watch to determine if he was on time, he assumed the terminal was just ahead. It had to be. He knew it. His sneakers hit the concrete. Left-right-left-right-slapping their soles in an endless, constant rhythm that might've been a beautiful love song if he was smart enough to create the lyrics. Marisole. Marisole. His heart called out to her as his gaze scanned over every terminal to determine hers. Blasted.

Why did she have to choose an airline so far away from the front doors? Only she would do such a cruel thing.

His heart yearned to laugh but his lungs struggled to breathe with every passing second. He always ended up last in grade school, lagging behind the others when it came to five hundred yard dashes and even longer runs. As much as he'd love to tease Marisole that she did this on purpose and chose the airline on the other end of the Earth to make him work for her affection, he knew that had nothing to do with her decision on choosing an airline. In fact, she probably had no clue he was chasing her, desperate to tell her he loved her though he had no idea what he would do after that. It wasn't like he created an organized plan of attack, steadily strolling through the airport to casually walk up to her and hand her a rose with affectionate words rolling off the tip of his tongue. He would be surprised if he had any air left to speak to her once he reached her. Maybe he'd pass out on the floor in front of her and she'd offer him mouth to mouth. In that case, he might not open his eyes ever again, on purpose. Maybe she'd forget her plans to leave and take him home, instead? He snorted. The obnoxious sound came out more like a choking guffaw. Jaws dropped and people cursed aloud, throwing their hands up in the air while he sprinted by them.

More than likely, instead of all the romantic scenarios flashing through his mind, he'd fall to the floor from lack of oxygen and intense pain generating from his upper thighs down to his wobbly calves. He would then be whisked away in an ambulance while she stepped foot on her flight, leaving him to lament all the years he spent aimlessly watching TV shows on his comfortable recliner when, instead, he should've been pumping iron at the gym, getting himself fit for an occasion like this. Damn his preference for snacks and entertainment.

Nooo! He spotted her stepping up to the doors which led her away from him. He willed his legs to run faster but they wouldn't budge. Instead, his traitorous stems slowed down.

He yelled but the sound came out as a croak. "Marisole! Marisole!"

He screeched to a halt, a person behind him almost running into him. They loudly cursed as he folded in two, placing his hands above his knees to fill his lungs with air before he shouted, "Stop! Please."

Clay lifted his head to look for her but it was too late. In the few seconds, he strove to collect himself and gain the ability to speak, the doors closed. The airline agent stared at him in front of the doors among a sea of faces surrounding him.

"Are you okay, buddy?" One man a few feet away from him offered his arm.

"Yes. Thank you." Clay waved his hand to indicate he was okay and didn't need help.

Damn it. What was he going to do now? She was gone. He stood there, stunned, speechless and trying to figure out a new plan. Marisole was on the plane. He had to do something quickly. Something. Anything. But what?

He shoved his right hand into his pant pocket and lifted his cell phone. Bringing the phone up to his face, he pressed the button at the bottom of the contraption and said in a stern tone of voice, "Call Marisole." He watched the screen as it dialed. His heart soared, the tremendous boulder pressing down on it, as soon as he realized she left, suddenly rolling away and allowing him to gulp down massive amounts of air while he waited to hear the one voice that could change the course of his future.

He had a chance.

She'd pick up the phone and he'd talk to her. By urging her to come back, he'd prevent her from making the worst decision of their lives. Please, Marisole, pick up. Let me talk to you. Let me convince you we have a chance.

His call went straight to voicemail. He blew out the breath of air he held in anticipation of hearing her voice and dropped his head in frustration. The boulder rolled back onto his heart nearly suffocating his insides. It couldn't be true. They were meant to be together. He held the phone in his hand and waited until her charming voice ended and the beep began.

"Hey, you. I miss you, already. Please take care of yourself. I wish you all the success in your new job."

His thumb pressed down on the screen to end the call while his heart urged him to say more. She was moving on with her life, starting a career in another state, and making a clean break for her benefit. He had to let her go.

Clay dropped the phone into his front pocket and started the way back to the car. If his car was still there, he knew he'd have some explaining to do. If it wasn't there, he'd have to catch an Uber to where they towed his car and pay a hefty fine. Regardless of what happened, it was worth it. At least he tried.

But it wasn't enough. Marisole was meant to be in his life. She belonged with him. He wanted no one else.

They were two peas in a pod with the same interests and the same values. He had to find a way to bring her back- to him.

The good part was they still had a connection. Joey would keep in contact with her even if she never contacted Clay again. Clay would get his life together, gain a career and, somehow, convince her to come back. He didn't know how but he would find a way to enlist her help and she'd be forced to step back into his life. Then, Clay would tell her all she meant to him and convince her to stay, forever.

For now, Clay was happy to remain friends with Marisole... Until they met again.

~The End~

A Note from the Author
If you enjoyed this story, please read the conclusion of Clay and Marisole's journey, New Home in the book ANGELS AND DIAMONDS.

Also By, TK Lawyer

(The Guardian League)
Jasper
Centurion
Apollo
Aeron
Orion

Stand-Alone Novels
Angels and Diamonds
Shifter Shorts
Serenade
Crossroads
Her Other Guardian
Nightfall

Anthologies
Love on the Edge of Danger:
A Pandemic Romance Collection

No Man Left Behind

CROSSROADS

About

PASSIONATE *PLAYFUL *PARANORMAL

International Bestselling Author, Tamara K. Lawyer, writes under the pseudonym TK Lawyer and was born in Colon, Panama. She moved to the United States with her family to pursue her post-secondary education aspirations and found her love of writing shortly after.

She writes sexy, heartwarming, paranormal and contemporary romances. Her books often toe the line, straying from traditional ideas to open reader minds and hearts to unlimited possibilities.

When she isn't reading or writing, she is likely spending time with her husband/best friend or catering to their lovable American Foxhound, Misfit, who steals all the attention in their house.

Connect with TK

Twitter
www.twitter.com/tklawyerauthor
Amazon
www.amazon.com/author/tklawyer
Facebook
www.facebook.com/tklawyerauthor
Website
https://tklawyerauthor.wordpress.com/

Milton Keynes UK
Ingram Content Group UK Ltd.
UKHW011940240823
427419UK00001B/18